COMPASS(ION)

HEART OF ELESARA
BOOK 1

GRAF
MAY

An Elesara Series Novel
Published by 252 Publishing LLC
901 Brutscher Street, Ste. D252
Newberg, OR 97132

This is a work of fiction. Names, characters, places, and incidents either are the product of the authors' imaginations or are used fictitiously. Any resemblance to actual persons, living or dead, business establishments, events, or locales is coincidental.

ISBN (Papaerback): 978-1-950753-10-9
ISBN (Ebook): 978-1-950753-11-6
Library of Congress Control Number: 2023910018

To Beast,
Hold your fire

For Hunter,
For philosophy, for history, and for the stars

INTRODUCTION

The following fictitious events take place in the
ALL Universes

and represents core foundation content across all timelines

1

WESTON

James Nukoin sat with his arm draped over the side of a modest ship. He had a thick leather book on a barrel that was being used as a table. The sails had carried them far east, away from Wyvern and around the southern tip of the continent. Soon, they would turn north toward Paisca and Angmaan.

Even sooner, he would run out of reading material.

They'd fled Wyvern a few days before, not a week before he would turn 17. At 17, his half-brother would find him and murder him to gain control of Wyvern. It was the way all kings gained power. James was the *lesser* of two heirs, his mother the unfavored mistress. His brother lived in the large house and lived a privileged life.

James was barely more than a slave (though, still more).

Wyvern was not his home anymore. The sea was vast on either side but represented hope. James watched as gulls dipped across the water and the sun bled against the twilight sky.

He would need a new name for his new life. Soon, he would find one he liked.

Along the deck, one of the crew of five walked toward them. He wore a thin woven shirt and loose pants, both made of sun bleached linen. He stopped before James' mom. "Excuse me."

His mom turned toward the crew member. She pulled her blowing honey-blonde hair away from her face, holding it in a pony-tail so the wind wouldn't whip it into her eyes. "Yes?"

"We're approaching the Gancanagh Island. It's best if you seek refuge below deck for the night."

His mom raised an eyebrow. "Are we?" She tucked her hair into the back of her pale pink dress with hand-stitched white and yellow flowers, and stood. She propped one foot on the lower rail. "James, hand me the telescope."

James offered it to her. She lifted it to her eye and peered out across the sea. "Which one is it?"

The crewmate looked at James, and sighed. "I must insist you get below deck."

"When I'm ready," she argued. "You can't even see it with the naked eye. I'm at no risk of being cursed by a Gancanagh."

The Gancanagh were male Selkies. Their gaze cursed any woman they met. If the woman's lust was rejected, even by miscommunication or a small hesitation, she would die from (irrational) heartbreak. They had all been given life sentences to a remote island at the far eastern end of the Selkies' island chain. There, the cursed men lived in isolation and the women—Selkies and magicless men—lived their life in safety, breeding the Gancanagh gene out of all lineages.

"What if one is out fishing?" the crewmate argued.

James glanced over the edge of the ship, wondering if Selkies occupied the sea below. There was nothing but waves and darkness.

His mom wove her free hand in the air, dismissing the idea. "Everyone knows Gancanagh are afraid of the water. I'm in no danger. The Selkies aren't dumb enough to come near the island either. Now point my eye toward it."

The crewmate sighed again. James offered him a shrug. "She'll get below deck sooner if you help her find the island."

The crewmate stepped closer and tipped the telescope a bit south of the eastern horizon. "About there."

"I don't—Oh!" His mom gasped. "Yes, there it is. A lovely little thing, isn't it? James, come look."

James stood, setting his book down on the table, and stood beside his mother. She helped him locate the island again. It stood as a small mound in the sea with a tall ridge running across it.

"Fascinating," James mumbled. "Will you please listen to him now? I don't need a new brother or sister."

"Fine," his mom groaned. "It's time for bed, anyway. You need rest too, and you shouldn't be on deck in Selkie waters."

"And yet you protest," he teased. His mom laughed while he gathered his book and telescope. He glanced at the crewmate, and with a small nod dismissed him. "Mom..."

"Yes, James?"

A strange feeling settled in James' gut. "Nothing. I'll see you in the morning."

She stepped closer, and then in a swooping motion pulled him into her arms and held him in a tight hug. "By morning, we'll be far enough from your father and brother's reach," she promised him. "I won't let them hurt you."

"By morning," James said tightly.

"James?" His mom's head peeked back out of the ship. "Should we open a gift early?"

"My birthday isn't until tomorrow."

"That's why I said early," she teased with a grin.

James glanced around, sorting why he felt so unsettled, but it gave nothing away. "That would be nice," he finally replied.

His mom smiled. "Wait right here." She vanished inside the ship and returned a moment later with a small box. "For you, my handsome son."

"Mom," James groaned. He set his telescope and book down then took the small wooden box from her hands and opened it. Inside was a small golden compass that could fit easily in his pocket. It had no letters, only a simple red tipped needle.

"What's this?" James asked. He looked at her, then back to the compass. "Am I supposed to add the directions myself?" The needle spun wildly until it landed toward the southeast. "It doesn't even work."

James looked up at his mom. She had been staring at the compass, but now she looked at him. "It isn't broken, James. It will show you exactly where you need to go."

James looked at it again. "It will?"

She nodded, then hugged him. "Happy birthday, James. My greatest wish is for you to see thousands more of them. A Luck Fae should live to 10,000. No less." Normal fae could live to 8,000, without the impacts of war and famine.

James leaned into his mom, still looking at the compass. "Thank you, Mom. For everything you've risked too. That was enough of a gift."

His mom swallowed, the playfulness gone. "It was the absolute least I could do for my son."

James nodded, cupping the compass in his hands. He looked up, out toward the sea.

He would be killed if he ever returned home.

"I love you," his mom promised. "Maorekel." *Always.*

2

KONRAD

"When a boy like you watches the stars, he loses sight of the worlds within himself," Ambrose warned. He slid the telescope out of Konrad's reach.

"When a boy like me watches the stars, he imagines the boat that would take him there," Konrad argued. The lens of the telescope caught the light of the fire as it spun away.

Konrad knew the night of philosophy, science, and sword-training was coming to an end. He continued to study the sky with nothing to aid him, save the lens of his own eye. There was so much more than this world, this island on it.

He reached his hand out as though he might touch the sky. Ten thousand years was a long time to spend in isolation: sabotaged, starved, and looked down upon.

Beside him, Ambrose chuckled. "Do you know why I still meet you, Kon?"

He didn't, though he deeply enjoyed their meetings. He did worry their meetings would end; that he might do something wrong, or he might come one night to discover that his mentor's tired bones had lain themselves down for the last time.

The man's skin in the moonlight rested in layers, each wrinkle a chapter of a long life lived in isolation. The smile lines around his eyes and mouth, the paper-thin backs of his hands—all of it spoke of the expansive mystery that was Konrad's distant relative.

Still, despite his age, Ambrose made the trek out here each week —for Konrad and for clear skies. The ridge sat a few hundred feet above sea, but it was the highest point and afforded the clearest view of the stars, especially when dense fog flooded the coast.

"Why?" Konrad managed.

Ambrose looked at him. The two of them stood there in the wind-rippled grass and gazed at one another, teacher and pupil. His eyes then glanced up to the sky. "You should get going."

Konrad's shoulders fell.

"Storm's coming in," Ambrose added. "You feel the way the air is building?"

The air was a swamp, with a slow warm current running through it. The storm would hit, the air would cool, and the sea would provide, filling the bellies of those who lived in the Stilts.

Konrad bent down in the long blades of grass and retrieved the fabric protector for the telescope. He passed it to Ambrose.

"Get on home," Ambrose advised. He slipped the telescope into its cover, propped it on his shoulder, and turned west. "I'll see you on Sendvish," he said before leaving.

They'd meet again, the day after tomorrow. After the storm.

Konrad stood on the hummock like a fool as the hunched silhouette made its way down into the valley toward the western side of the sea, toward civilization and satiety. Toward those who had banished Konrad and others like him, who dared love a man in a world where they would never lay eyes on a woman again.

When the man vanished, Konrad turned east and jogged. He had a long ways to go, fifteen miles before dawn. At the rate Ambrose walked, Konrad suspected he would be at the Stilts before Ambrose reached the main village.

He ran down the hill, up another, and through the low trees at the crest. He ran down that hill and across the salt bog, and finally up the ladder to the home he shared with Khale.

Despite that the sun slept, Khale had already woken. He had stretched their tattered blanket neatly over their thin pad of vines and straw. In the space's center, Khale stood over a low fire. The warmth bled across the room, not quite reaching the edges of the space. The scent of boiled potato and vegetable soup twisted Konrad's stomach in tight hunger.

The sight of Khale leaned over the pot in the half-light, his ruddy red hair like an ember beside the fire, awoke other instincts in Konrad. He stepped up behind Khale and kissed the back of his neck. "Morning," he murmured in Khale's ear. He tucked a strand of Khale's hair back.

"Morning," Khale said, louder. He turned to face Konrad, the cast-iron pan still grasped in his left hand. He'd wrapped the end in an old tunic to protect his hands from burning. "I made breakfast."

Within the pan was a small measure of soup so thin that each pasty vegetable—there were seven—showed like a shadow in the fog.

Khale offered him the entire pan.

Konrad's stomach rumbled.

"Did you eat?" he asked Khale.

"This is the last of our ration," Khale said—unnecessary words. Konrad tracked their food nearly as carefully as Khale did. They'd seen their food supply dwindle over the last few weeks until it was down to nothing.

Khale's hand left the pan as he turned fully toward Konrad. He grazed the skin of Konrad's lips, a light kiss. "I'm not hungry, and you ran."

He tasted of hunger, which is to say that he tasted like nothing but himself—not the faintest trace of food on his lips or his breath. Konrad deepened the kiss. Only Khale would make such an offer.

"Eat, please," Konrad insisted as he pulled his mouth away from Khale's. When Khale didn't move, he insisted: "We'll catch something today."

"You know you need it more than me," Khale protested.

"Khale," Konrad said in a low murmur.

"We'll split it," Khale said. Konrad could hear in his tone that Khale wouldn't argue further.

Konrad nodded. "Alright." He divided the contents of the pan evenly between them, drifting the vegetables between an invisible divide. To appease Khale, he gave himself the remaining vegetable. To appease himself, he gave Khale the three largest vegetables.

Khale's smile grew as he caught what Konrad was doing, but he did not comment.

Konrad raised the pan in a mockery of a toast. "Would you like your spoonful first or second?"

Khale laughed. It was a low rumbly sound that kept Konrad warm on the coldest nights and kept his hunger at bay on the worst days.

"What are we trying to catch?" Khale asked. "No one has caught anything in months."

It was true. Today, Konrad knew, would be the exception to that trend. Ambrose had known it too; it was why the man had sent him home without finishing their conversation.

Konrad walked to the paneless window and held open the shutter to reveal the scarlet sky beyond. "Blood sky," he stated as Khale walked to his side and peered toward the sunrise and the sea. "We're due for a storm. It ought to bring fish."

He heard the relief in Khale's next expiration before Khale uttered, "We need it." He ran his hand over Konrad's cheek, resting so that his thumb just touched his right commissure. His fingers knotted themselves in Konrad's hair. "Did you enjoy your night?" Khale asked.

Not as much as he intended to enjoy his morning. Or perhaps his afternoon, or the storm itself while they were trapped in their home, hoping that the battering waves of the ocean would not critically compromise the integrity of the stilts on which their home stood.

He focused on the task at hand: survival.

It meant forcing himself to step away from Khale for the time being. They would have hours alone together while the storm raged. Now was the time to rig something to capture anything interesting that washed up in the surge.

"We should be ready for this weather," Konrad said.

"Maybe our house will finally blow away," Khale mused, his fire opal eyes alight with his humor.

Konrad laughed.

He loved Khale's eyes, which despite marking him as a Gancanagh were deep and expressive. They shared his humor and his thoughts without any movement of his face.

"If it washed us to another shore, that wouldn't be our fault. We could have bread," Konrad mused. However he tried, Konrad couldn't make it sound like the joke he'd intended it to be; it was a deep longing in him.

It was a longing whose fruition would be met with a punishment worse than his fate on this island: Death—his and any woman he happened upon.

"You're not worried about killing someone?" Khale asked, serious and soft, mirroring his thoughts.

Konrad swallowed and moved his hands together in front of his chest, his mind buried in thoughts of a confession to Khale.

Khale would understand and never judge.

"It's difficult to care at times," Konrad admitted. He stared at his bare feet while he said it, but now that the words were out he met Khale's eyes, assessing. "They don't have that same concern with us."

"What's the value in living like this?" Khale asked.

It was a powerful question with an answer Konrad loathed to dwell on. Life without purpose was hardly even existence.

3

WESTON

James Nukoin had spent his first 17 years aware he was Lucky, but he had only recently begun to realize he had the worst sort of Luck. As far as magics went, his was unruly and often inaccurate. It didn't tell him to avoid the boat or that this trip was a bad idea. It also didn't indicate anything was going wrong on their journey to safer shores, like it did with the many earthquakes or tornados that made his homeland more dangerous than the sea. It did, at least, wake him up with a sense of dread moments before he otherwise would have drowned. It did, at least, seem to want him to live.

He sat up in his bed, his heart throbbing. He let his feet hang over the edge of his bed, into the pool of water that had flooded his cabin. His stomach churned. It was a small cabin. The natural wood of the ship lined the walls. There was a single bed built under a porthole window and a closet built into the other side of the wall, with an iron latch that ensured the doors didn't fly open during travel. Soon, the entire boat would be part of the sea, where corals and algae could fight for dominance among the curved boards.

Luck, for lack of anything else, kept him calm and focused. Or perhaps that was the adrenaline. He forewent socks and shoes. Soon, he would be in the water and those would only weigh him down. He fought off the urge to brush his unruly blonde waves, again because he didn't have time nor purpose to look good. Who would he impress? He didn't want to attract a Selkie nor an Undine. He opted only for a shirt and pants, something lighter that he had been saving for Angmaan's hot market. The outfit would flow easily in the water. He grabbed the compass his mom had given him and tucked it into his pocket. He clipped the string into the fabric of his pants, making a small hole to ensure the compass was secure.

He opened his door and left the room, his heart thrumming so hard he could hear it louder than the whooshing of water as it toppled over the boat's deck. He saw no one, heard no one. Had they forgotten him when they'd abandoned the ship?

He was desperate to find his mom. He flung doors open as he moved through the boat. Cabin after cabin lay empty.

"Mom?" he called in the halls. He was running out of time. He wove his way toward the surface of the ship, pushing against the walls so he wouldn't topple over as the ship tossed from side to side. "Mom!"

The crew was Undine—able to breathe in the water should the ship completely succumb to the storm. His mom had Luck.

Their Luck was not the kind of luck that prevented your ship from capsizing in a storm or avoiding it entirely, but it was the kind of luck that saw you through it alive—the kind that could tell you what choices to make. Hopefully, hers wanted her alive too.

James walked up the last set of stairs into the whipping air of the sea. It was now or never for him.

"Mom!" he yelled one last time, but no one responded. He doubted anyone could hear him, either.

The air howled past, whipping his shirt tight against his chest. The pants were too thin, and the air cut through them, filling them like balloons.. James grasped the rope that lined the side of the ship. He worked his way toward the side of a ship where he knew there was a boat he could get on. He made his way, his feet slipping with each wave of water that splashed over the side of the ship.

"James! Get off the boat," someone yelled from the sea. "Now!"

James covered his eyes with his hand, his arm arched across his brow, and yelled, "Where's my mom!"

"She's gone!" the man yelled back. "Go!"

James mustered his strength and let go of the rope. He reached for the small rescue boat, only a dozen feet away, but a wave crashed down, engulfing him and flinging him down the boat.

He closed his eyes and focused on what movements would be more perilous for him, what movements might give him a chance. He focused on his life. He could sense how low his odds of survival were, yet he clung to them with every ounce of respect for his magic he could muster.

What if Luck hadn't warned him because he needed to be right there, in that moment, sliding off the ship into the tumultuous sea?

Surely his father couldn't track him if his ship had sunk...

He took a long, slow deep breath. He pulled his shoulders away from his ears, willed his body to let go of fear. When he let go, the boat and his body went opposite directions. Wind slammed him into the crest of a wave. The wave crashed over him like a snack.

You are a tenedol balel, James. Your life is in danger. His mom's voice echoed in his mind. He opened his eyes, desperate to grab her, but it was a memory. She was nowhere. The waves threatened to consume him.

He held his breath while his throat strained and his chest whined with need. He knew if he let the salty brine sting his lungs, he would be in more trouble. If he held his breath until he felt the wind whip his skin, he could survive.

Standing on the precipice of life and death, he had little to reflect on. There was nothing to see, and even if there was, he doubted he *wanted* to see it. Creatures from the deep hungry for a meal, Selkies hungry for fresh blood once they'd mated, or even simple jellies drifting in the sea...none of them appealed to James. All he wanted was to see the sky above him, a shore ahead.

The seconds passed in slow motion. He wasn't sure fighting for his life was worth it—though his instincts pushed him on. To suffer for a short period felt like a tradeoff, a risky tradeoff considering survival would mean his father would still hunt him. He had to escape the ascension ritual, escape being sacrificed.

The water curled its cold endless arms around him, threatening to pull him into the abyssal depths his worn, spasming muscles could no longer save him from. He was at the mercy of Luck.

To die at sea would be to deny them the satisfaction of murder. Murder was essential. His half-brother would never become king without a body, without a convincing argument that he was responsible for James' death.

To die at sea would be noble.

His brother couldn't become king as long as James lived, no matter *how* he lived.

For that alone, he had to survive; he had no choice. Fate had dragged him to this moment, these seconds that beat at him and transformed him without his consent. If he pulled through, broke the crest of waves and gasped the crisp air, he would find a new identity.

The seconds ticked on. His lungs felt like explosive balloons, ready to burst. His throat threatened to let in the briny water against his will. Still, he did not fight the water. Luck said patience, Luck said wait, Luck said he could survive this if he did exactly what it said.

Luck was a bastard.

Suddenly, wind ripped across his cheek. Tears stung his eyes. He gasped for air, filling his lungs as quickly as possible in case another wave took him under. Furious waves slapped against his body. He was in an endless rotation of free-floating turmoil. Now, Luck said he had to fight. He tore at the water relentlessly and with no sense of accomplishment. If he hadn't had Luck, which he now despised in many ways, he wouldn't have known that each stroke he made was moving him forward—moving him toward something that felt hopeful and destined.

His parents had always said he was on a path for great things. To his mother, those things meant living and freedom. To his father, they meant sacrifice and death. James hadn't cared about his destiny before. He had never given much thought to mortality, either. He did value Luck, flawed as it was. If you felt like something was a very bad idea, you didn't do it. If it was anything you felt shy of, you did it. James knew, now, that there were only two choices left in his life: to die as a great *disappointment* or to find his destiny. Not the ones they had prescribed for him, but the one that made his soul sing and his heart burn with fire.

If he survived, he would have to defeat his brother. He would have to end the legacy of tenedol balels—inheritance keys—for a better future.

He let all these thoughts pass over him as he wore his muscles down, as he approached what he hoped (and trusted) was a shore.

He felt the future path before him—like an endless stretch of incandescent creatures guiding him toward safety.

He missed his mom already. She had been soft and secure and someone to seek in moments like this. She'd defied everything to save his life.

There was one choice, one possibility: On this, his 17th birthday, he would survive.

4

KONRAD

They'd cut the thin trees. They'd woven the net. They'd climbed into their homes, and they'd ridden out the storm through the afternoon and into the night.

Now it was a new dawn. He and Khale descended the ladder, one after the other, and took in the destruction. A thin band of light crested along the horizon. Through a thin fog, Konrad took in their small village: Debris coated the sand—broken shells, some sort of sea plant with bubbles that looked as though they might pop but wouldn't, sticks, sea rocks, and pieces of old shipwrecks.

Three of the buildings had collapsed. The detritus from their walls lay across the ground and all over the stretch of the strand which contained the stilt homes.

One of the other villagers, Urial, approached them. His beard had begun to turn more salt than pepper, though his hair was still mostly dark brown. His gray eyes, flecked in a rainbow of colors like all Gancanagh, matched the sea today. "You're safe, then?"

Khale answered for both of them. Konrad appreciated the response; it meant he didn't have to say something unnecessary like, yes, *we're alive*. Were they not talking to Urial? Why would he ask such an unnecessary question?

"Have you found anyone who isn't?" Khale asked Urial.

Konrad glanced at the collapsed structures.

"Daxon and Weyblor," Urial said. He gestured toward the farthest collapsed building, where one stilt remained upright. Last night, they'd slept there, unaware that they were moments from being crushed or drowned.

"Marn," Urial said. Marn was older and lived alone at the end of the line of structures. He never seemed to resent the life they had, and he'd survived there long enough to grow old.

"And Gunnar," Urial finished, with a nod toward the final structure. It belonged to Goran and Gunnar.

Konrad swallowed back his reaction and reduced it to little more than a shared glance with Khale. Gunnar had been the only fire fairy among them. He could turn the soggiest driftwood into kindling. He kept them warm, started their fires, and cooked their food...

Gone.

Casek came over. He and his lover Magne were the newest residents of the Stilts. Their bodies were young and healthy. They hadn't felt the strain of a winter season yet.

They still felt entitled to the basic amenities of life, things the rest of them had learned to live without. In some ways, Konrad envied them. More often, he grieved. As they moved through each phase of acceptance, as they took on the challenges of their future, each member of their little community re-lived his own transition to the punishment they faced together.

Konrad had no patience for Casek now, nor for his demanding lover. They would not feel the losses in the same way the rest of them would because they had not known them for more than a dozen weeks.

He cleared his throat. "We're going to see what washed up," he declared. He lifted the disk-shaped basket to his waist and embarked on the trek down the strand.

"If you work from that end," Urial suggested, "we can take the nets down as you go."

That was wise. The sooner they removed the vines and set them out to sea, the lower the likelihood that anyone from the village discovered their newfound technique.

"Do you want me to help take it down or collect?" Khale asked Urial.

Khale had a way of seeming to be deferential while he used his helpfulness to get what he needed. The artistry that went into the skill impressed Konrad.

"Five should collect," Magne announced. An unseen string seemed to draw his chest further away from his body as eyes cast themselves on him. "The rest should pull down."

Magne cared more about safety than the harvest from the sea. Konrad tightened his grip on the basket.

"Says who?" Urial argued. "That's too many pulling the vines down."

"How long did it take to put up?" Magne countered. He let a silence eat at the minds of the company before he pressed, "We need everyone we can spare."

Konrad ignored them all and focused on Khale's hand on his shoulder, warm and sure. He felt Khale's hot breath graze his ear an instant before Khale whispered, "What about rebuilding? Gunnar is gone. We'll freeze if the last fires go out. At least one of us should tend the fires."

He nodded and whispered a reply: "We'll need to have a place for drying grass and sticks."

"Drying?" Casek mocked. "Nothing's drying in this weather."

Of course not. It was damp and overcast. A fine mist fell over everything. They would need a hot day to dry the kindling and a dry place to store it. With the seasons changing, that weather was becoming more unlikely.

"If we made a canopy between four trees," Konrad explained, "we could set things out in the sun."

"Who put you in charge?" Urial asked.

They would argue rather than accomplish anything, and waste the morning. That was alright. Konrad could use the mental challenge to keep him alert.

"I should be in charge." That was Goran. He'd lost Gunnar. In his mind, Konrad set aside a day or two for Goran to grieve before anyone expected him to be a capable man again.

It would be more than just a day or two, if Konrad ever lost Khale. It would be an eternity spent wandering without a tether, caught in some purposeless wind.

Perhaps he ought to allow Goran a week.

"I'm one of the oldest," Goran reminded everyone.

If they were to survive, not this week, but their own average life expectancy, they needed to solve the larger problem, not argue about smaller ones. Konrad met the eyes of the group one at a time, a tactic he'd learned from Ambrose. "Do you know why societies ostracize people like us?"

"I suppose you think you do?" Urial scoffed. The whites of his eyes showed briefly before he shared a look with Magne.

"Because we are murderers," Goran supplied. Either he was being deliberately abrasive, which would never surprise Konrad, or he was too addled with grief to understand that the question was based on rhetoric, not on seeking an answer.

"Because," Konrad explained, "we supply no genetics. We bear no fruit." He meant gay men in general, and he hoped that message came through. "But... No one on this island is reproducing."

From that standpoint of societal progress, if the society on this island would never bear its own fruit, why ostracize the few who did so by choice rather than by punishment? What difference did it make?

Nothing, save that it gave those in the village someone to sneer at and horde food from.

"So what does it matter?" he asked them all. "We can convince them we have skills to offer, items we can give them to trade for food."

It was optimistic, but he didn't think it was unreasonable. Neither did Ambrose.

Magne laughed. "And they take all the items and give us nothing!"
So why waste the effort trying?

Sometimes Konrad felt as though he lived among savages and not in a society of merchant's and craftsmen's sons.

"Perhaps," he agreed with a nod of his head. He needed to be calm, to present this in some way that would make them want to agree.

He needed Khale to be the one doing this, not himself, but Khale was so tender and shy in his mannerisms that Konrad would never ask it of him. To speak to a group of angry men, grieving men, with conviction about their futures...

"I'm doing something productive," Goran muttered. He swung his basket onto his hip and headed toward the nets.

Konrad followed. "I may be wrong," he confessed to Khale as they walked toward the far end of the net. "But I may be right. I wish they would listen."

Khale ran his hand down Konrad's back. "You should be our leader. The village leader listens to you. You have good ideas."

Konrad barked a laugh of surprise. "If Ambrose listened to me, we would have better lives. I'm not leading." Look at the way the group responded: exasperation, amusement, anger. Not one of them showed a level of respect. He was merely Konrad, with the wild ideas.

"I'll challenge them for you," Khale insisted.

Konrad wasn't sure what he meant by that, but he misliked the idea of Khale challenging anyone. He liked him soft and safe.

Konrad faced him. He cupped his jawline along the heel of his palm. "I love you," he said with a kiss that Khale returned. "Challenging isn't the way. They have to want it. They have to think it's their idea."

They went back to work for a time, filling their baskets with fish and seaweed and sticks. After a while, Konrad puzzled aloud to Khale, "As long as we have needs and wants, they have power."

"How do we stop having needs and wants?" Khale laughed. "We're already starving."

Khale's sentence, he concluded, could be roughly translated to *as long as we're alive, they have power*. He didn't want to die, especially not by the slow emaciation of hunger.

He needed to stop going to see Ambrose. It consumed too much energy. He couldn't bear the thought of losing the one thing, besides Khale, that gave him hope and purpose in this place.

He couldn't convince Ambrose to change the food allotments, to sway the people to allow them to hunt. He allowed them to starve. Allowed them to die.

"The dolls should help," Khale said, in answer to his own question.

Konrad hoped so. He reached for another fish and then hesitated. There, tangled in the debris, was a hand. It twitched.

Konrad glanced down the strand, where someone had lain out the bodies of the dead. One, two, three, four, five. All were there.

"Five," he muttered aloud. "Then what..."

He reached toward the hand.

A foot or two away, something—some*one*—coughed.

"There's someone in there," Khale commented, with a surprise that mirrored Konrad's.

There was also hope. If they rescued someone from the village, perhaps he would feel beholden to their family here.

He grabbed a sharp rock from the beach, and together he and Khale worked to cut away the vines and sticks surrounding the person. Konrad peeled away a layer of seaweed to reveal a young man.

If he was a villager, he was new. Perhaps he had been on a boat on his way here.

Konrad slapped his face gently. "Waken."

The man came to.

His eyes.

He wasn't Gancanagh. His eyes were a clear muddy green.

"I'm alive?" the man asked. He flipped a lock of hair the color of a plover's wing feather off his face.

Beside him, Khale softened. "You are for now," he told the stranger. "How did you get here?"

"The storm destroyed my ship. My mom..." he looked around at the desolate beach. "Is gone."

Every man here shared the loss of their mother. Commonalities such as that one were dangerous lines of thought when Konrad needed to see this man as nothing more than a tool.

His agenda changed: If the man wasn't Gancanagh, then saving him would matter to people off the island. Perhaps they could use him to campaign for better treatment.

"I'll check the rest of the vine," Konrad offered. He knew Khale would make the man into a project, and the newcomer needed the sort of emotional support Khale would provide. He didn't need someone gruff like Konrad. "Get him into the house."

"She's not in the vines," the man said confidently, as though he could somehow know. Perhaps something had been done to her before the ship went down.

"What makes you certain she isn't there?" he asked.

He shrugged and then winced in response to his own movement. "I just have a feeling. Don't waste your time. It's only me."

He was another mouth to feed, and a new complication of somehow getting an injured man across the island. Konrad's eyes surveyed the line of vines waiting to be harvested.

"Perhaps we shouldn't have wasted our time on you either," he pointed out to the man.

"He doesn't mean that," Khale said quickly. He gave Konrad a *look.*

Khale would have made a natural father, someone skilled at nurturing the best traits in his children.

Konrad ought never to have a child.

"I get feelings," the man explained. "You can check, but I know she isn't there."

Feelings. Konrad ran his hands down his face, considering. There were magics he didn't know of. He'd been surprised to learn of Gunnar's fire magic years ago. Perhaps this man had his own magic.

"Where are you from?" he asked. "You're not one of us."

"Nivern. It's east. We've been sailing westward for days."

He knew Nivern on a map. It was, quite literally, a piece of rock with sheep on it.

"Useless in trade," Konrad muttered to himself. There wouldn't be any Nivernese merchants passing through, eager to find this lost person or reward those who had saved him.

"Why are you traveling?" he asked.

"We're merchants," the man replied. Konrad let out a low chuckle as the man shifted. "Headed to the desert port: Angmaan. My mom didn't want them to go around the south of Klith during storm season."

"Can you work?" Konrad asked. Perhaps he had useful skills to teach them.

"I don't know," he answered with another shrug-wince. "Maybe. On some things."

In other words, no.

"What's your name?" Khale asked in his gentle tone.

"Don't ask its name," Konrad groaned. "If it has a name it has a personality." If it had a personality, Khale would grow inevitably more attached. Life in the Stilts was unforgiving, resources stretched thin. There was no circumstance in which keeping him here would end well.

"If it can work it has a personality," the man argued. Joked? Did he make a joke just then? "Even if it's only a horse."

Konrad laughed. The man was far too likable. He would bring them nothing but grief. Why had he come here?

"Alright then," Konrad begrudged. "What's your name?"

"Weston Akhan."

Another difference—Gancanagh were stripped of their last names when they arrived at the island. It was a part of the process of removing their identities. Long ago, Konrad belonged to the merchant house of Selig. His promising future vanished the day his eyes changed from blue to the black fire opal which marked him as Gancanagh.

Weston Akhan. It was a strong name.

"Besides your cuts, have you any injuries?" he asked.

The man coughed in response.

Konrad tallied the lacerations on his arms and legs. The man was lucky his neck hadn't snapped while he was caught in the vine.

"I think I broke my leg," he complained. He bent and pressed his hand into his calf just below his knee.

"You're walking on it," Khale reassured. "It isn't broken."

"Well it hurts," he said.

Konrad wondered whether it was a sprain, a deep bruise, or a subtle fracture that could withstand the man's slight weight.

"It's going to keep hurting until we get you to the other side," Khale warned him. He gave Konrad a grim look; having the man attempt the trek across the island would be a chore. And then they'd have to leave him. They'd have to trust the people who punished them to care for him.

"You mean until I die," the man said. His voice was solemn, eyes downcast.

"What makes you think you'll die?" Konrad asked him. Weston. He had a name.

Not that Konrad cared.

"I think there are high odds," Weston said. He touched the palm of his hand to his own forehead, the way a mother might do.

It was such a compassionate gesture. Konrad had lost so much of his merciful side since coming here. It was a wonder, probably Khale's influence, that he had any left whatsoever.

"Having a feeling?" Konrad asked, amused.

Tendrils of friendly affection grew toward the man. His naivety made him feel young—like someone they could tend to. He fought the tendrils as the three of them walked toward their house. It wouldn't do him any good to grow attached to someone whose loss was inevitable.

"It's a long walk," Konrad warned. "Does your feeling think you'll make it or will we need to carry you?"

Weston crossed his arms and walked off-balance for the sake of proving his determination. "I can make it."

"Finish the vines," Khale urged Konrad. "We'll be at home." His eyes scanned the waterline. "They'll be here soon."

He was true. Already the sun climbed above the horizon.

"Why is everything so ominous here?" Weston complained. "*The*

23

other side," he said in mockery of Konrad's voice, *"they'll be here soon.* Are you sure I didn't die?"

Konrad chuckled.

And then, to his surprise, Weston angled his body to face them, eyes wide. From his pocket, he withdrew a foil-wrapped packet. "I didn't steal the bread. I was going to give them back. But, I thought I might need it..."

It couldn't be possible. Food. Civilized food, not food which had been hard-won but food that had been lovingly prepared, likely by a mother.

"You have bread?" Konrad asked.

Weston reached into his pockets and pulled out a small package. It was likely not watertight, but nearly so.

Konrad took it from him, unwrapped the wax-coated paper carefully so that it might be repurposed, and tore the bread in half. It wasn't a salt bread, but a sweetbread, with cinnamon swirled throughout. He passed the larger portion to Khale.

"That was *my* bread!" Weston protested.

Konrad offered the sweetbread to Weston in an exasperated apology.

Stealing food. What had he become? Was he more animal than man now? Where did he draw the line?

Weston looked at the bread, licked his lips, and turned away. "You need it more," he decided. "There's some stuff in the vines you may like too. And...the wreck might attract some big things. You need a small boat."

As if they could simply obtain one at the local market.

Konrad took a bite of the sweetbread. He'd forgotten the deliciousness of sugar.

"We need many things," he told Weston.

Rather than chew the bread, he allowed it to sit in his mouth, full of flavor, until it dissolved. He took another bite and watched as Weston limped off ahead of them.

He smiled, amused at the man's willpower.

"So where's this house?" Weston asked. "I hope it has a good sea view."

Konrad laughed and wrapped his arm around Khale's waist. Today they had bread. Today they had a young man, new to this world. He watched a fire of longing for family in Khale's eyes as they followed Weston. A protege might serve them well, fulfilling Khale's longing.

If it were in his power, he would give Khale a son. He'd never seen Khale want something so much. If only they could keep Weston...Konrad would keep him for Khale's sake, teach him to survive, and take him under their wing.

But for Weston's sake, he needed to leave the Stilts, get off the island, and return to a home with a future.

"It has a view," Konrad promised Weston. He kissed Khale's cheek in remorse at his inability to give him what he longed for. "We'll see to it that you've returned home safely," Konrad told him.

Weston looked at them. "Okay. If you can get me there, I can give you somewhere to live."

Konrad ignored that for what it was: an impossible promise.

Khale squeezed his hand. When he let go, Khale and Weston made their way back to the house.

Konrad returned to his harvest.

5

WESTON

James walked into the camp with the man named Khale. Konrad continued to harvest from the sea nets, while he could. James believed both Khale and Konrad had been honest about their names, even if James had lied: He wasn't James anymore, not to them and not to the future. He was Weston Akhan, a name he'd made up because they'd been traveling west and because akhan meant 'kind' in Elesarian. Kindness was a trait he hoped to emanate. A trait his father lacked. Weston Akhan was a good name—something he could remember and something he could adjust to. It was the kind of name he almost wished he'd had all along. James Nukoin had died. He would not be missed, except by his brother. His brother would never ascend.

Luck would help him respond when he needed to, until it felt natural to hear Weston and turn his head.

As for the appearances of his new friends, they looked exhausted and wet. Khale had shorter messy reddish hair, while Konrad had long wavy near-black hair and a full beard. They seemed to match in most other ways, from their shorter height to the way they walked in tandem. The more Weston walked through the village of broken houses on fragile poles, the more he realized it was a look shared by all residents. It was the weight settled onto their collective souls. It was despair.

It was a strange place. It seemed like the poorest of towns Weston had heard of, but there was no apparent reason for them to be poor. They were near the sea with nets to collect food. They had an island of resources. Why wouldn't they utilize them?

"Where did you grow up?" Khale asked him, looking down toward Weston as they limped across rocks and through puddles.

"Nivern," Weston replied. It was the name of an island off the coast of Wyvern, where he'd truly grown up. It was home to good people, the kind of people who had helped his mom and him escape. The kind of people that would lie and assure Konrad and Khale they knew a Weston Akhan if the time ever came.

Secrecy wasn't going to be easy with Konrad. He had looked at Weston with a knowing gaze that bore through the lies. The lies would have to be delicately crafted, rooted in honesty, but with subtle, memorable, twists. The men had already become aware of his magic easily. Between their observation abilities and the desperation of the land, Weston knew his survival depended on friendship.

Being alone with Khale felt like the best opportunity to have conversations about Weston's roots. He had to keep some secrets, even if he felt he could trust them, even if he needed to become their friends. He knew he couldn't trust them with everything, and he could sense there were others nearby who would be a danger to his life—others who would sell him to his father if asked the right question.

The house Khale stopped at, entered, and expected him to enter looked perilous. It was nothing more than twigs strung together to form something some might call walls, and others might call a fishing basket. The whole contraption sat at the top of a rickety ladder. If the construction wasn't questionable enough, it was perched atop twigs in the water.

Weston looked up the hillside. There were thick trees in the mountains. There were *mountains* they should have been able to live in.

The house was tall enough for someone under six feet to enter, but neither of the two men was very tall. Luckily, neither was Weston. Inside it felt claustrophobic, with the walls coated in mud as insulation. Weston was used to living better, even on the ship.

The space itself was filled modestly: a bed that fit both men, a small area to cook beneath a fire, a two-person table. Khale pulled one of the chairs from the table and motioned for Weston to sit. He got comfortable, his leg propped on a crate, as Khale pulled a container of water out from beneath the bed. He pulled the second chair in front of Weston and sat, the water on the table and a ragged piece of cloth in his hand.

"How many people were on your ship?"

"There were five on the crew, my mom, and me."

"You were traveling to Angmaan?"

Paisca "Yes," Weston replied.

Khale lifted Weston's leg, watching his face for any sign of agony. Weston relaxed into the chair. His leg would heal quickly at least.

"I don't know where that is," Khale said. "From here... how far away?" Khale asked.

"It's about halfway from home. I don't know much about sea travel. This was an educational trip."

Khale nodded and dipped the rag into the water and began washing the sea and dirt from Weston's leg. When he pressed the rag deeper into one of the wounds to pull a chunk of coral out. Weston winced, his teeth pressed together and his hands balled into fists.

Khale worked in silence mostly, and Weston tried to find something to look at. It was a boring room, but it was new. It was also somewhere important, somewhere that represented something. Whatever that was, Weston hadn't developed the keen mind to ask the right question to sort out why. A hierarchy issue must have prevented them from better living, but asking the precise question was what Luck demanded. You had to know exactly what to ask to get a solid feeling. For the time, he just memorized as much as he could: each speck of dust, each board that looked too soaked to withstand his weight, each twig in the fire that was supposed to warm the place without burning it down, without sinking through the floor and falling to the sea.

Then, the door opened.

Khale didn't look; it was like he knew. Weston tried to relax, hoping Khale would be alarmed if it wasn't someone he knew. Then again, in such a small community, they likely knew everyone.

"A chest washed up, along with what we believe is part of a chest. Any idea what might be inside?" Konrad asked him.

It hit Weston with a force he wasn't expecting: homesickness. He wouldn't be home for a very long time—and only if things went well. He might never see anything he knew again, neither familiar land nor face.

He was alone now. His future was in his hands and a bit in the hands of the men who had found him.

He wouldn't see his mom again, the captain, his dad, or his siblings. They were his past.

"Food," he said. He looked at them, their sparkling eyes of reds and blues and other colors that made them unique shining back in wonderment. "Probably."

He knew he should keep better tabs on his magic.

"Probably?" Khale asked. He pulled at a piece of skin on Weston's arm. He felt his flesh peeling away from him, unveiling a hot, pink wound.

"Ouch." Weston tried to yank his arm away, but Khale held his wrist in place.

Weston stopped. He could tell they were just trying to help. He looked at his arm and saw blood droplets falling. This wasn't even the worst of it. It looked bad, but he knew he was in store for something worse. He just wasn't sure what yet.

"It sounds like it looks like a food chest," Weston clarified.

"No feelings about that?" Konrad asked.

Stop figuring me out. Someday, he would trust them completely and tell them the truth. Konrad, more than Khale, would be his friend. Konrad was important to his future. But what did that mean for Khale?

Khale wrapped a clean piece of linen around his arm to form a bandage and then set his hands on his lap. He was kind and gentle and deserved to have as bright a future as Konrad would.

Weston looked into Konrad's glittering eyes. "I *feel* like it looks like a food chest."

Konrad grinned, a small laugh escaping his lips in an exhale. "Alright." He looked at Khale. "We'll dismantle it carefully to preserve the wood."

"You know, it's interesting you think it looks like a food chest since you haven't seen it," Khale said.

Weston looked at him. "I said it sounds like it looks like—"

"But we didn't describe it."

Weston exhaled. All food chests looked the same, and he knew it was a food chest. It was welded shut and constructed well so the water (and kids) couldn't get in it. It would be full of lots of things to eat once it was broken into. It didn't look like any other chests, nor fracture like the partial chest, because water wasn't as big of a problem with other chests. The idea was to keep the box watertight so if something like a shipwreck happened there would be food (if the box made it).

He explained as much to them. There were several more unaccounted for boxes of food. Some could make their way to the island.

He felt it like a rippling of knowledge—another two chests would make their way to the island. Luck wouldn't let him starve, at least.

"And that is why I suspect it is a food chest," Weston finished. "Based on the limited description that it was not in pieces."

"Tell us more about your feelings," Konrad requested. He made it sound reasonable, but it alarmed Weston. "Can you guess what this place is?"

He knew there was no escape from the island. He knew they were being punished for some unknown cause, and not allowed to use resources for some unknown reason. He knew they were being starved deliberately, but not quite starved enough to die.

He suspected they were being drained of the will to live.

"They're just feelings." The words left him with force and fury in a heated race to avoid the scrutiny.

"No ideas?" Konrad pressed.

"How would I know? It's a..." Weston let the sensation overcome him. Instead of lying, he felt pulled toward telling the truth. He was tired of this destiny stuff.

He studied the two men. He knew they were south of Angmaan on an island. He knew their eyes were strange. He knew only one race to have exceptionally unique eyes that twinkled like fireflies on a deep dark night: Gancanagh.

The Gananagh were marked by their eyes, but they were cursed to form a deep and erotic attachment to any female they encountered. They would lock themselves away until a pregnancy was achieved, often for weeks. Throughout the next several months they would still be insatiably attached. It was a curse to lock the Selkies down, because with their seal skin they were prone to ignoring their maternal instincts. Instead, the men raised the children, breeding again anytime their wives returned.

Gancanagh were meant to be a solitary race, spread out over thousands of micro islands, except the Selkies had rejected a life of insatiable attachment to a male, and so they had imprisoned the Gancanagh on an island. If they bred, they bred Selkie females and human males. No Gancanagh would see the world again.

If they were Gancanagh, they were here to die. The fish would be protected resources of the Selkies. The waters would be off limits. Harvesting would be...

He couldn't resolve a reason against allowing them to farm.

However, he knew his mom was not there because it would have been bad Luck. She would have been forced to stay, forced to carry a Gancanagh child that would be fated to the islands or killed.

It gave him hope; his mom could be alive somewhere else. Alive and safe.

But, if they were Gancanagh, the compass...Weston felt the weight of it in his pocket. Had it been warning him?

"An island just for men. Men who have your eyes," Weston said vaguely.

"Are we killers?" he asked.

"Some say you are." Each of them had cursed a woman, and had killed them.

"But not intentionally," Khale stated, iterating what Weston already knew. Weston rolled his eyes.

"Will we hurt you?" Konrad asked him.

"No," Weston groaned, his voice sinking as he spoke. They wouldn't hurt him. They were boring people who did boring things when they weren't busy starving under archaic laws. Their lives weren't exciting or adventurous. They just accepted that the women were controlling and wouldn't let them exist freely.

Weston liked strong women, like his mom, but he hated bossy women, like his grandma. She was the kind of person who believed in the dreams of Maelchor—that princesses had pieces of his wife's soul and were all married to Maelchor first.

Weston wasn't going to marry some princess person, so his kids could have Maelchor's wife's soul in them. That was gross.

"So you can trust us; you should stop lying. It doesn't make friends with men like us," Konrad said.

He wasn't *lying*. He was avoiding things.

Weston swallowed. He needed them on his side. He needed their friendship to survive. He felt it, coursing through his future like threads on a tapestry: Konrad, at minimum, would be one of the most important beings in his life. Khale...There was a darkness there. Weston shied away from it and met Konrad's eyes. "I have magic."

Half of Khale's mouth made a smile, and half of it stayed straight and almost twitchy, "Do you?"

"Luck magic. Really dumb Luck magic."

Khale laughed. Konrad didn't.

"Why is it dumb?" Konrad asked.

"Because I'm here? My boat sank. I shouldn't have been on it, or I should have known to get off it before things became dire. Or..."

He knew he was meant to be on it. Lucky people didn't have sinking ships., unless the sinking was planned.

"Yet you are alive," Konrad pointed out. "That is the beginning of

Luck."

And he was the ending, Weston could tell. Not romantically. Weston blinked away. Konrad was married, and Weston was destined to marry a woman.

"I said dumb luck, not bad luck."

"If you have Luck magic to protect you, and it seems to have failed you, then perhaps you do not have all the facts." Konrad ran his hand through his hair and looked around the room. He stopped on Khale, who offered a warm smile before saying, "Misunderstood luck?"

Weston inhaled sharply. *I'd love to see what you could do with Luck. It would be impressive.* Maybe giving Luck magic to Konrad was part of the way forward. Konrad could be the ultimate weapon against his dad. Konrad could be the person he needed to meet.

"We're supposed to meet," Weston stated. "So my boat sank to get me here."

Konrad glanced at Khale and then back to Weston. "Why?

"You know, Luck doesn't have conversations with me," he replied.

Konrad's lip twitched into an almost laugh.

"I'm not helping someone without a plan," Konrad said dismissively. He turned to look out the hole in the wall that stood for a window.

They were at an impasse. They had no idea what they had, but he bet Konrad had an inkling about Weston's value to others. Still, they were silent.

Finally, Konrad rubbed his fingers through his beard and asked, "Why should we care about you?"

"I don't know," Weston replied. "It's just a feeling. I'd like to not deal with it, personally."

This time Konrad did laugh. The two Gancanagh men looked at each other, their eyes locked in one of those mind-speaking things. Weston didn't get how it worked, except that he could guess until he got it right, and then he would know. They couldn't do that, but they seemed able to communicate without words. Maybe enough years together with the right person would create that sort of unspoken connection.

"It might be best if you keep that feeling, in particular, to yourself," Konrad decided. "Perhaps all of your feelings. Some of the men in our company struggle with foresight."

Weston sighed back into the chair. "I will tell you what feels safe. Starting with the food: There were several chests of it. You should find them and hide them before the sun sets."

Konrad looked at Khale, "You should tell the others. It shouldn't come from me."

If Weston had to work with someone forever, he liked the idea of Konrad. He seemed to flow with Khale. He was intelligent and careful. If they could work together well, Weston had hope his future would be free—not just of his father but of the island. If they could work well together, they would all be free.

A rush of excitement filled Weston. The next few days would thread the line of life and death, but he felt the future unfolding with possibilities.

"When are we hiking?" Weston asked.

"What are your injuries?" Konrad asked him back.

There isn't time for healing. "I'm getting sick," he told them. "I can feel it settling in. The cough that kills people."

"Is it going to kill you?" Konrad asked.

"I don't know yet," Weston replied. He didn't think, so because he could still see a future beyond this place. "I can sense options for my future, which can't exist if I'm dead, which means I probably won't die. But I might."

Konrad nodded, "Dead men don't rule."

"I never said anything about ruling," Weston said, but the words sank in like honey in the sun, oozing into Weston's being: he would be king.

"Tomorrow night I meet with a friend. He'll take you the remainder of the journey," Konrad said.

"What about you?"

Konrad shook his head.

But you're part of my future.

6

KONRAD

Homes in the Stilts offered limited reprieve from the unbearable afternoon heat, which wasn't so much sun as it was a bog made of salt and air. They passed around an animal hide with fresh water for drinking, to keep cool.

They'd shared stories for an hour—the young man, about the world and his childhood and horse farming. Konrad and Khale shared some of their experiences before coming to the Gancanagh Island. Neither felt the need to share about their life since arriving, though it seemed self-describing.

Now they heard a bell. Weston straightened. "Is that the dinner bell or something?" he asked.

He was hungry, most likely. Konrad was.

Then again, Konrad was always hungry.

The bread this morning had caused an ache in his stomach. It had been so long since he'd had sugar that his body didn't know what to do with it. He hadn't asked Khale yet, but he suspected they would both be sick in a few hours, if not sooner.

He rested a hand on Weston's shoulder. "It's your way out of here, earlier than expected. He turned to Khale. "You should speak with them. I'll only anger them."

Khale kissed him. Konrad felt the tension in his back and biceps, the tightness of the muscles that outlined his ribs.

"I will," he assured Konrad. He turned his attention to Weston, firm. "They're scholars, or so they claim to be. You shouldn't advertise your abilities."

Konrad imagined the worst of the egos from the village if they discovered what Weston was capable of. The way they would put him to work, the advantages they would take...

He considered other options as well: using Weston as a shield, as a means of going to the mainland. It would be simple to avoid women with his talent warning them whenever they were at risk of meeting one. He could run errands. If they used him in the same way, Konrad and Khale could have a life.

But no. Konrad knew the grief of a life in captivity. He wouldn't inflict that on another, however it might ease his own future.

And Weston would inevitably turn on them. He may be young now, but they would have thousands of years on land, working to contain and control Weston, in order to protect others from their curse.

Better that they starve here than trap him.

"Yeah, I got that," Weston said.

It took Konrad a moment to realize he answered Konrad's words and not his thoughts. If he could hardly be trusted with Weston, how could others?

"Do you?" he challenged. "They could hide you. No one would know they had you, and they could keep you as a slave. You should be as unintelligent and dull as possible."

"They don't want me," Weston insisted. He descended the ladder.

Khale glanced at Konrad, worry written on his brow. Hope, too. Worry and hope were such a strange combination, yet the two emotions seemed to work in tandem so often.

"Good," Konrad called down the ladder after Weston. "Then they'll send you home."

He and Khale followed after him. The three of them on the ladder at once caused it to sway and creak in new ways. Konrad, caught in the middle between them, enjoyed that challenge. His hands were calloused enough that they did not suffer.

One of the men from the village, Florian, stood along the vine. It wasn't fully dismantled yet. They'd decided, with the fog, that it wouldn't be visible from the waterline, and so they could catch more in the coming days and replenish their stocks of smoked meat for as long as they could keep their fires alive. Despite their hopes, Florian's foot dug into one of the vines lying along the rocky shore.

Florian was about six hundred years older than Konrad with auburn hair and a clean-shaven face. Unlike most liquors—not that Konrad had enjoyed liquor in his life, he simply knew the reference —Florian had not improved with age. The Village could have sent anyone. There were plenty of contented people. They'd sent him.

Konrad wondered whether they'd sent him because he volunteered or because he needed someone to spit on.

"What's this?" he demanded. His face puckered toward the vine.

Konrad held his sharpened stone in one hand, dull side against his palm, just in case. "Some debris tangled in the stilts. We're working to remove it."

Florian's eyes turned toward their house, pointedly. "You seemed like it," he said, all sarcasm.

Some others from the Stilts stepped out of their homes, watching from a distance. None of them cared to treat with Florian, it seemed.

Khale stepped forward. "A young man washed ashore." He moved Weston in front of him and rested his hands on Weston's back. "He needs to be returned home. His ship sank, he claims. He is not Gancanagh."

Florian first checked Weston's eyes, inspecting them for any hint of Gananagh, Konrad assumed. Then his gaze settled on Khale's hands and their resting spot.

"How many of you had your way with him?" Florian wanted to know.

Konrad took a few steps away, hands on the back of his head, and breathed out his anger. The assumptions, the implications...he was so deeply exhausted of it all, so badly outraged when they resurfaced.

"None," Khale said. He had a mild way of speaking, which reduced any chance of Florian responding with something else clever and cold.

"You think they're animals?" Weston spoke. "Do all men *have their way* with every woman they meet?"

Not that Florian would know the answer to that. Nevertheless...

Konrad turned to face Weston. "You're a very stupid boy, aren't you?" he reminded him. He didn't need Florian, of all people, taking an interest in Weston.

Weston's jaw settled into place, set against whatever words he longed to say. He held them in check.

Khale pushed Weston towards Florian. "He needs passage off the island. We can prepare items to trade for his fare. Dolls."

Florian backed away, waving his hand in a dismissive manner. "No one wants your used whore. Even his parents won't want him."

Perhaps, if they sank Florian's boat, they could get away with killing him and blame it on the sea.

"His parents are dead," Konrad snapped. "His mother, at least."

Weston looked down at the sand, pretending to be patient and dull.

Konrad willed him to be a rock—as uninteresting and useless as he could manage.

Weston angled his face toward Florian. Light danced across Weston's eyes. "You could check my body and see," he offered. "But that would make you like them, wouldn't it?"

Damn the boy.

Konrad saw the tension in Florian's muscles before he lashed out at Weston, but not soon enough to do anything more than stop the boy's fall. Weston's face would have a nasty bruise from that. It did not seem as though Florian had managed to break his nose.

"What's in the box?" Florian asked Khale.

"His dead horse," Konrad supplied, before Khale could say whatever he intended. Anything from *We're not sure* to honesty would lose them the box.

"I'm a horse breeder," Weston explained, pride evident in his tone. "Best horses around. We breed them. We chopped off my horse's balls and froze them, to deliver to a king."

"What in hell is a horse?" Florian scoffed.

Rock, boy. Be a rock.

Instead, Weston goaded with a smirk. "It's an animal you ride." He did not say it as though it were a beast of burden. He said it with heavy implication which left a deliberate vagueness about the use of the word *ride* in this particular case.

Florian's face puckered again.

Weston stepped toward him. "So when do we leave?" he asked. He was suddenly very genial, as if the argument of the past few moments had never occurred.

"You'll be sentenced here like the rest of them," Florian decided. Konrad knew a single story from Florian would be sufficient to turn the village against Weston. "We can't let people like you out."

Florian picked up one of the baskets of fish and seaweed harvested from the vines and dumped it into the water.

"Thank you," Konrad said. He mirrored Weston's tone. "We were too weak to discard that ourselves."

Florian ignored them all. He dragged his boat into the water, climbed in, and rowed further out to sea.

Konrad scowled after him. "Sometimes I think I'd like to kill that man," he told Khale.

"You should," Weston said. Konrad couldn't decipher whether that was spoken out of rage or as an ominous warning. Weston went to the water's edge and pulled the fish back into the basket. In the rocks, he found a shelled animal that tended to live in deeper water. "Look! Food."

Khale breathed out an excessive amount of air. "Why don't we open that chest," he suggested. "We could make a feast."

"Alright," Konrad agreed. He scooped what he could of the floating food into his hands and returned it to the basket.

Tomorrow, he promised himself. He'd meet Ambrose and explain about Weston and see that he was cared for safely.

Tomorrow.

7

WESTON

The chest and a basket of fish, one they'd managed to hide from Florian, were still sitting there after hours of debate and an entire day without food. Weston felt like he was starving. He had no idea how they did this day after day. The largest issue was the inability to decide what should come first: Bury the dead or cook the fish.

There was a deep fear someone would return from the other side of the island, and it wouldn't do Weston well to tell them their worries were unfounded, for the day at least.

He waited, his eyes drooling and his mouth held shut with the last reserves he had, trying to contain himself.

"It'll be good," Weston said. "Better than ship food."

"Our last meal was watery soup with a handful of vegetables," Khale stated from beside him.

"Khale has small hands," Konrad said.

A small handful would only be a few pieces, not enough for one person let alone two.

"Then you'll really like this," Weston told them.

Finally, they dismantled the chest. They tore at it piece by piece, removing chunks of boards to circumvent the lock. Inside, there were dehydrated and pickled meats, vegetables, and fruits. The assortment was mouthwatering. Instead of bread, which would rot too quickly, there was ground wheat and corn. There was also an assortment of spices. The scent wafted through the air, transporting Weston home. Beneath the spices sat a bundle of toffee wrapped in waxen paper. The thought of buttery sugar blend made his mouth water.

His stomach growled. He should have paid more attention to cooking as he grew up. So many skills he'd never developed, never imagined he would need. For one, he was supposed to die. His life was meant to end by his 18th birthday. The hunt began at 17. For another, he was a prince. He had little use for basic life skills.

Khale began sifting through things. Weston noticed the way he cataloged each item, counting them in reference to the living. Nothing would be unequally distributed.

"Who said you get to keep this?" the guy who had opened it asked.

"We're sharing," Khale said, reiterating Weston's valuation of his morals. He stood taller than the other guy and looked at him with command.

"Suddenly you're in charge?" another guy spat out.

Not suddenly. He'd heard Konrad and Khale's comments; he'd seen the gentle urging Konrad was doing to see Khale rise in their community.

Weston could have learned the names of everyone, but he didn't think he needed to. Konrad and Khale were the figures that mattered most to his future. He let them be various figures in his head, defined by voice and appearance and role. The first guy was the grumpy one, and the newest guy was the challenging one.

"He's a better choice than I am," Konrad stated.

"You were the only choice?" a third guy said. He had big rings around his eyes as if he wanted to sleep forever.

"I'm in charge," Khale stated.

The rings guy laughed. "And the kid?"

Weston was a man, not a kid. He may be the youngest man there, but 17 years was nothing to laugh about. He'd made it to adulthood, and then a year further.

"Florian put Khale in charge because I mentioned we'd been arguing for days," Konrad told the group. "Weston stays. For now."

"Everyone watched that conversation. You're lying," the rings guy said.

"Watched?" Konrad asked.

This wasn't going to be productive, and then no one would eat; not the fish nor the food in the chest.

"If you let him lead, I'll help you," Weston said, hopeful his comment would end the pointless argument. He flipped a rock into the air, the one Konrad had dropped as soon as the boat guy had finished insulting everyone to feed his own ego.

"How will another stomach to feed help us?" an old guy asked.

"I've barely arrived, and you have more food already," Weston pointed out. "I know things. I know the shipping habits of the area."

He didn't *know* them, but he could guess somewhat accurately.

"You think men who watch the sea don't?"

"Then why don't you?" Weston retorted.

They continued to argue, mostly about the rules Florian had made and the finite details of their social system, especially since they'd lost so many men. Weston wanted to eat and be alone. This island was the antithesis of alone. He would have to set out and explore to experience solace, but if they were all here on the coast, there had to be something dangerous inland. Perhaps more of the other Gancanagh, or perhaps a monster?

Luck didn't differentiate, but generally agreed it wasn't safe.

Then, at long last, an idea settled on him: "Could you use someone with earth magic?"

Weston hated his using his earth magic. It was from his father, and marked him as Nukoin. There was a line between disowning your family and disowning yourself, and Weston supposed if earth magic would help, he would offer it.

Khale looked at the group, instead of Weston, so he knew it was a good idea. "There are salt caves he could give us access to."

"Yeah," another guy said. "There are. If we traded, we could hide what we got down there."

Hadn't Weston suggested trade, not five minutes before this moment?

"And how would you build a boat out of our rocks and sand, boy?"

Weston looked around. "The mast needs good wood. You can use your houses to hide it."

"How?" Khale asked.

"A detachable float. The boat can be reattached to a house to disguise it."

"We have these flattened homes. No one needs them, save Goran," someone suggested. "Plenty of wood."

The rings-around-his-eyes guy looked up, and Weston guessed he was Goran by his sneer. "Go ahead. Get yourselves killed."

One of the guys who had been enthusiastic about the salt caves offered to help, and a few others pledged themselves too. Some left the area with Goran.

Once everyone had settled down, Khale took stock of the volunteers. "Good," he said. He held up a basket of fish and some cornmeal from the trunk. "We'll make a community meal tonight with whatever embers are left in fires. And someone will guard the fire at all times."

Weston watched with interest until Konrad and Khale began talking. He took the chance to sneak off up the banks of the village and off behind some bramble, limping as he went. His breathing was already labored, his chest heavy. He knew they didn't have anything in the camp to heal him, but he hoped he could find a plant that would have some medicinal properties.

Exhausted by the climb, he let his body collapse against the steaming earth. He let himself be. He was mostly alone now. Whatever he brought together in his own life would be new and his.

They still hadn't eaten.

8

KONRAD

They had a party with the food. It was a one-off; they wouldn't be able to eat like this again. But for the first time in centuries, Konrad felt sated. It reminded him of the time they'd managed to snare a few dozen gulls. The villagers had taken the snares away, but for a few weeks they'd eaten well.

It was one night—one night where everyone in the community was content. They built a raft from the siding of one of the collapsed houses and rowed each of the dead out one at a time in the dark to be dropped into the water. They used vines and stones to weigh them down. Goran had prepared Gunnar's final voyage and a special eulogy.

They prayed over the bodies, for Maelchor to take care of them.

They prayed over the food, in thanks that Maelchor had delivered it to them.

Konrad could never decide how he felt about Maelchor. He spent much of the night with his gaze on the stars, his mind on Ambrose and on Weston's future. Ambrose was a deeply theological man, who searched the world for evidence of some sort of grand design. For his part, Konrad decided that either Maelchor was an all-powerful god —who had chosen to have children banished to isolation on this island—or he had watched fairies do so and chosen not to help them.

Either way, regardless of whether the stories about Maelchor were true in a historical sense, Ambrose insisted they were true in a spiritual sense. That they gave a person guidance and direction and a sense of belonging to something more.

Konrad had once convinced Ambrose to deliver a shipment of scrolls to the Stilts, so they could learn the ways of Maelchor. They'd repurposed them for sanitary needs and used the wood bars at the center of the scrolls as a means of preparing animal skin to become clothing.

Following his discovery of the use of the scrolls, Ambrose had given up talking to Konrad about Maelchor. He kept his conversations and musings purely on the scientific side of things.

Konrad missed the Maelchor discussions. He felt Ambrose had shared more of himself in those days.

At some point, one of the older men, Vas, took up a song—one of the old songs from home about a powerful Gancanagh who drew his Selkie love home from the sea. It was a tragedy, as all such songs were, but Konrad found himself singing along. He loved the old tune.

When the last low moan stretched out over the sand, marking the Gancanagh's grief for his lost Selkie bride, Konrad felt a chill by the fireside. This was brotherhood. These men were his home. They may fight. They may all starve slowly at the hands of those who fed off the power they held over the Stilts, but they were together. They were one.

Urial met Konrad's eyes across the fire. He tapped his hands on the empty air, and Konrad nodded. Together, they went around to the houses, collected the cooking pots, and passed them around the fire. Those without pots took sticks.

Urial started with the basic four-step beat for rowing. Their race was known for its prowess with speedy transit across the sea. Where others used sails, Selkies employed oars, manned by men and women alike, with one person in the center calling the beat.

Once Urial started the four-step, Oain added something more

complex, and the rest of them joined, one by one. All they needed was a fife, rising above the beat, and a line of dancers kicking together.

Konrad glanced at Weston to see how he liked the music, and his hands faltered in their movement. The newcomer sweated. He was pale and damp and coughed far too much.

With alarm, Konrad looked to Khale. Khale, he knew, had been attentive all evening. Where Konrad had taken the opportunity to enjoy himself, Khale's focus had been on Weston: ensuring he ate well, ensuring he sat upright, ensuring he remained close to the fire.

"He needs to be seen by someone," Khale murmured. "Does your *friend* have any power?"

"Tomorrow," Konrad told him. He worried that tomorrow might not be soon enough. But Weston seemed alert enough. They'd make an early start—leave by mid-morning to allow for the likelihood that Konrad would carry him much of the way to the meeting with Ambrose.

Konrad rested his hand on Khale's thigh. "He knows medicine," he assured him.

"Do you think he's safe by the fire?" Khale worried. His eyes wandered over Weston's resting form.

Konrad knew all three of them would spend the night by the fireside. He kissed Khale, wished he could promise impossible things like Weston's survival, their own departure from this island, and meals like this every night.

"Safer than in our house," Konrad mused. "The fire eats the dampness."

Khale nodded his head in agreement. He leaned into the crook of Konrad's shoulder, Together they watched Weston breathe while drums beat out an endless pulse in the night.

9

WESTON

The wind blew fiercely through the night. The Stilts swayed, the wood threatening to crack against the strain. He'd found no plants to heal him, not in the vicinity of the Stilts. Weston blinked awake, the air caught in his throat, unwilling to fill his lungs. He was beside a fire, exposed to a clear star-filled sky. He wasn't sure when he had arrived, or why he was there.

He wasn't sure he was sane or what was what anymore, except that he knew he was on an island. His ship was gone, his mother lost at sea. He let the feelings navigate him through the mess: No, those were trees, not monsters with large swirling eyes. Knots. They were knots, deep-rooted into the spindly tree trunks like the pain of losing everything.

The fire was hot—not hot enough to feel good, but hot enough to burn him if he rolled into it. With the draft, he almost thought burning would be an improvement of things. Almost.

He blinked again. The trees stilled; his body was the one swaying like a log trapped in a narrow pathway of water.

"How are you?" a voice asked, covered in the shroud of darkness.

Weston contemplated it. He didn't think about his own being often. He liked to think of games to play and lessons that mattered. He liked to think of horses and valleys. Instead, he was on a desolate island of moisture and misery. There was little else than himself to think of.

His chest felt full of grit.

"My chest feels like I've reached the Angmaan desert." He coughed, the feeling of sandpaper grinding against each breath. "It feels like the closest I'll ever get."

"We'll see you there," Konrad replied.

Would he see him there in death, or would he see to it that he got there? He suspected either would be fine, in the end. He had, in feeling, aged a thousand years while lying there in agony, his chest shaking with chills and burning in an inferno.

Konrad had been studying him. Weston met his gaze and tried to smile, though he doubted it looked like much more than the pained exacerbation of withholding a cough.

Weston turned to cough into the ground, and as he did, Konrad sat beside him, his legs folded. "When I was young, I wanted so badly to leave my island and see what else the world contained. I know that drive. How it feels to look at the stars and wonder what other worlds are sharing the view."

"You'll see the world again," Weston assured him. It felt true. They would see the world. Weston blinked as his body shivered.

"Your feelings are very optimistic. I have neither the means nor the conscience to allow that."

Weston rolled toward the flames, gazing into them as he coughed. The fire moved with each hack of his chest. He wouldn't last long without help.

"There's a way," Weston said. "Do you know where my sister's dolls are?" he asked Konrad. Why were his sister's dolls on the ship? She hadn't come with them. He looked around at the pieces of wood and bits of blanket that crept out from underneath him. The heat returned, pounding at his chest. He couldn't see straight. He tried to focus on the fire.

"This feels like a riddle. Where?"

He tried to pinpoint how Konrad was supposed to get off the

island; he couldn't make it past the incurable thought that it would only be Konrad. He searched more. Somewhere out there was an answer.

"Somewhere here," he said, settling on some unidentifiable source of safety from his magic. "I don't know."

His chest tightened, and he felt the building pressure inside of it. The seawater he had swallowed while swimming had set the path for the fluid to wreak havoc on his system. He didn't want to die here, on this island, with so much else to live for.

He closed his eyes and let images of home fill his mind. He was too fixated on home. He wasn't sure what else to think of, though; he missed his home, even if he could never go back, not unless he was prepared to stand against his brother and father.

"They're on the island?" Konrad asked.

Weston looked at him, through the raspy convulsions. "What?"

"You said the dolls were somewhere here."

"The way off the island is on the island. I don't recall if I have a sister. I don't know where the dolls are. I asked you."

Konrad stared at him and then rocked back to give his legs room to stand. He picked himself up and left the area, leaving Weston alone to his thoughts and the feelings of time poorly spent. He wanted to swim another direction, toward somewhere easier than this island. Somewhere with less despair. It was unsettling to be surrounded by so much suffering. Why did Luck want him here? For his own funeral?

He wanted to make this place better, but it wasn't his place to heal.

Konrad was back. Weston's thoughts flew away with the wind that had carried them there. "Will you sit?" Konrad asked.

Weston pulled his body to a seated position, though the constriction on his lungs was a new level of unpleasant. Simply moving upright was a workout in itself.

Konrad had brought Weston a wooden bowl of broth: warm water with the light flavor of fish, vegetables, and corn. Weston had never eaten food so plain in his life. Still, the liquid pooled in his throat and filled him with momentary solace from the ache.

"How long have you been here?" he asked Konrad.

"Just shy of a thousand years," he replied.

"Do you remember home?" Weston asked.

"Well." Konrad cleared his throat. "It never leaves you unless you want it to. You won't lose sight of yours even if you wander before you return."

Weston felt the stretch of distance and years lying before him— from that moment until the one where he would be reunited with the sheer cliffs and rocky shores that adorned Wyvern's cost. He would be older, wiser, and braver.

For now, he drank his broth and listened to the hymn of the Gancanagh, a melody that struck his soul with the solidarity of this community.

It would stay with him, like his home, these moments and this place.

Weston let his body sag as the bowl emptied. The heat cooled. Time and song ended. When the land had grown silent, except for the splash of waves upon the shore and the shuffling of feet as they found their way to bed, Konrad spoke again. "It's more sheltered than this island. This is what they call a break-water island. It is hot at my home."

"I thought it was plenty hot today," Weston joked.

Konrad chuckled. "Yes, it was, today."

"We're the same, you and I. Nivern is rocky and cold, harsh—with earthquakes and tornados. My home is jungly. Thick vines, endless fields of grapes and vineapuls."

"Wyvern is your first home?" Konrad asked casually.

Weston wasn't supposed to have told him that, but it was done. If he died, none of it mattered, so he nodded. "Yes, though I like Nivern. I like it here, too. If it was dry, if you could live on the hill in safe shelters, if you had food...it would be nice."

"They don't allow us food. They are powerless against the Selkies, but here...here they have power over us."

Weston let out a long, "Ahh."

Konrad was quiet.

"Were you banished because you love Khale?" Weston asked.

"Yes," Konrad said tightly, shifting. "We all were banished here for preferring a man's touch. The others see us as less than human"

Weston managed to set his hand on Konrad's knee. "I do not see you that way."

Konrad hesitated, then let a small smile settle on his face. "You may find yourself in the minority."

"I must have landed on the right side of this island," he joked. "What was your home like?"

Konrad looked up at the stars, his eyes pulled from the mix of all colors, fighting for dominance, to a more muted red and tan combination that lulled Weston in and out of the world that surrounded him. "Tropical—like Wyvern perhaps. The fog rarely goes so far. I miss bread the most. And girls. I wouldn't know what to do if I saw one now, I think. What is your favorite thing about home?"

Girls, Weston agreed. Girls like his mom and his sister and the various other women who filled his life with contentment. Girls who didn't demand he die for power.

"The waterfalls," he said instead. "In North Wyvern there is a great waterfall that spills from atop a bowl-like crater. It pours into the valley where a town was built. I was born there, even though I grew up in South Wyvern. I miss the thundering sound that called us home. You could hear it a mile away."

"Does the sound of it relax you?"

The sound of it was thunderous and loud, more calamitous than the sound of the waves rushing onto shore or his ship breaking at sea.

"No," he replied. "I just like it. Hooves relax me. I love the sound of a herd of horses galloping across the land, their feet racing against the ground as they move as one. I'd like to own a thousand horses one day."

"Will you tell me more about your feelings?" Konrad asked.

"Which?"

"How it works; why you trust them."

That seemed like an odd question to him. Why wouldn't he trust them? He had always trusted them.

His boat had left him in this place, though there was hope at the end of this portion of his journey. There was hope stretching far into the future—hope that could end in this fever.

"It's who I am," he said. "It's called Luck, but I think that's the wrong name. We're called Djinn. They're a type of slave: slave to wishes, slave to Luck, slave to what they can do for others. But we're not much better than anyone else. When you want to do something, you have feelings. Mine are just more accurate than yours. I can control them, ask them things, and search through them. Plus, good things just happen to me. This," he referenced his body, sticky with sweat, "aside."

Konrad's chest rumbled. Weston's wheezed.

"Like becoming king," Konrad said. He pulled himself to standing again. "Would you like more soup?"

Weston did want more soup. He had hardly eaten and the soup did not sate him.

"I don't think I can. No. And, maybe a king. I don't want to be one, but I might not have a choice."

A feeling settled over him with the word *king*. They formed a layer of nausea over the existing misery that entirely ruled food out.

"You'll be king. You know that," Konrad said.

"I wish I could give you Luck, so you could tell me that with your heart." There were few ways to gift magic, and most required attachment.

But, Weston wasn't sure he wanted to trust his instincts if they were going to lead him through misery. His mom had been a guide. He needed one, a hand that would help him make hard choices.

"Tell me what you feel when you think about it," Konrad prompted him.

"Scared," Weston admitted. He tried to clear his throat, to take back the confession, and found himself trapped in the pain of another pounding repetition of coughs. "Bright."

Once it stopped, and his gasps for breath filled his lungs again with the hope that this was not his last few moments, he pulled his shoulders back as best he could and raised his chin. "It's not certain. It could tip either way like your houses."

"Alright," Konrad said.

"Our houses are stable," Khale said, settling beside Konrad "Regardless of how they look, they've withstood many storms."

Weston laughed through another coughing fit that burned his throat.

"Let's get you to the meeting place now. We may end up waiting, but we can go," Konrad decided.

Weston looked around. Surely it wasn't morning already.

"Okay," he replied. He pushed one foot under the other to stand.

"Do you prefer to walk or to be carried?" Konrad asked him.

Weston looked out and wondered where he had been for the past day. Had he lost time?

"Has a man ever told you he prefers to be carried?" Weston asked.

"All men become boys when they're weak," Khale said. "It never leaves, and comes out when you're most vulnerable."

"I'll walk until I can't," Weston said, knowing that time would come too soon. The first bit of travel would be uphill, though. The least he could do was make it through that part for Konrad.

Weston pulled himself to standing with Khale's help. He liked Khale. He didn't like the way Khale's future felt. He smiled at him, though. "Thank you."

"Alright?" Konrad asked.

Weston glanced around. "If I die...what will you do with my body?"

"In our culture, we bury at sea," Konrad informed him. "Like the others, you will be too."

"If that were my fate, I wouldn't have bothered to swim to shore," Weston replied as he took his first steps toward a small path that wove into the cliffs.

Khale cleared his throat.

Weston froze. He took a deep breath and turned back. "I think I'll see you again," he assured Khale, but he hugged him nevertheless. "I'd like to."

"As would I," Khale replied. Khale looked toward Konrad and then back to Weston. "I am happy to have been able to. I hope you are successful—that you get home."

"We'll be moving more slowly. I ought to be home by midday tomorrow," Konrad told him.

Khale pulled Konrad into a tight hug. "See that he doesn't come back. That he gets home. Even if you have to see to it yourself."

"I'll bring you a stone from the other side of the world," Konrad promised. With that, Weston turned away to give them privacy. He worked his way up the hill, his head throbbing with a painful headache. *One step*, he reminded himself. *Then another.*

The last thing Weston heard was Khale uttering the words, "Be safe," before Konrad was beside him, supporting his arm where it was more slick and steep. With Luck, Weston managed to keep his footing. Within a few hours, they were at the top of the first crest and greeted with several other peaks ahead—a wave of land that occupied the center of the island. They made a decent pace through trees and along a winding path that was narrow and somewhat overgrown. Weston could tell it was used. He followed the earth, minding stones and pausing too often to catch his breath. It wasn't long before it was too much for Weston, too far to carry himself. Konrad lifted him into his arms before he asked and began carrying him through the heart of this hell.

Konrad didn't seem to mind.

Weston didn't either, after all.

10

KONRAD

Because he trained with swords under Ambrose, Konrad had enough muscle mass so the trek across the island, carrying Weston much of the way, didn't fatigue him. It did dehydrate him, especially with Weston's burning fever against his body, but he knew a route that passed over several streams. Even though it was longer than a straight path, he took it to preserve his health.

He arrived at the meeting place at dusk, in good time despite the longer route. Weston lay unconscious in his arms, so Konrad found a tree to lean against and propped himself up with Weston upright against his torso and waited. They'd still beat Ambrose.

The moon had made about a quarter of its trek across the sky when Konrad heard a twig snap a few yards away. A moment later, Ambrose crested the hill. He took in the site of Konrad sitting against the tree, of Weston held in a near-sitting position.

He sighed. "I heard there was a boy." He sounded tired and old. The span of the thousands of years between Ambrose and Weston was hard for Konrad to imagine. Here were these two, from such different ages in time, meeting.

He needed to dispel whatever rumors Florian had spread about

Weston. "I'm not sure what Florian told you, but he's ill. He needs medical care and passage home."

Ambrose sighed again and looked skyward. Perhaps in thought or prayer. "Florian complicated matters." He met Konrad's eyes. "The final merchant ship of the season left late yesterday."

They'd likely remained in the harbor until the storm passed. If they were gone without Weston and word got out to the merchant families that a young man had been found and not turned over for the full winter...

The entire island could be punished for Florian's actions. If those in the village suffered, Konrad's group would suffer more.

"For a leader, you're bad at it," Weston contributed.

Konrad hadn't noticed that he was awake. His eyes remained closed, but the words had been sharp and clear.

"He said you had an impetuous manner," Ambrose ridiculed softly. He set the telescope in the tall grass, protected by its fabric cover, then turned back to Konrad. "I'll do what I can for him. The others won't accept him."

Weston straightened as Ambrose bent over, hunched with age, and peered into his eyes. "Beautiful," he murmured. "Tell me, boy, what makes you sick?"

"Fluid in my chest," Weston answered. He was wise enough to be direct with Ambrose. Or perhaps not; he added, "I got lucky and survived a shipwreck, only to live long enough to die from something else."

"Have you made your peace?" Ambrose asked him.

"No," Weston said, dismissive and amused with himself. "I've made a few enemies, though.

"You should ask Maelchor to prepare you for your journey. He guards the souls of those who follow his ways, to shield them on their journey to the land of the dead." Ambrose rested his palm over the boy's sternum. "May I?"

"You're not allergic to outcasts?" Weston murmured. He leaned his body back against Konrad to give Ambrose easier access. "Why do you help Konrad?"

"I help him because he needs it," Ambrose said.

Konrad kept his disappointment in check. He would never find out, at this rate, what drove Ambrose to encourage these meetings. He didn't intend for them to stop, but it would have been nice to know there was something there, even if it was nothing more than a mentor's love for his student. Love of any sort could do powerful things in one's psyche.

"But it's your fault he needs it," Weston argued. "There's an inequity between the sides of the island."

"How can you know that?" Ambrose muttered. Shock colored his tone.

Konrad found himself examining Ambrose's countenance in surprise. The way he asked his question led Konrad to wonder whether there might be more to their friendship than he understood.

"He told me about the island," Weston explained. "You're the leader. You sentence them to their miserable lives. Starve them. How can I not know?"

Ambrose deflated slightly, relaxed into an easier state. "A leader only has the power his people afford him," Ambrose explained. "They're not ready for the change; I'm not able to force it. I'm sympathetic to the needs of all the islanders, which is more than my replacement is likely to be. I'm old and tired." He turned his head to look at Konrad. "I should have stepped down centuries ago."

Konrad and Ambrose had shared this same conversation so many times that it was like an old footpath in his mind, familiar with soft dirt and no remaining snares.

He watched as Ambrose placed his finger on the bare skin of Weston's chest and tapped it with the finger of his other hand. This emitted a faint hollow sound. Ambrose repeated the technique, moving his finger all around Weston's chest and back as he listened.

Konrad heard it when the sound changed from hollow to dense and dull. His eyes met his mentor's in the dark; Ambrose didn't think the boy would survive. He could see it. Not that he needed to see it to know. Ambrose had already told Weston to make his peace.

It was a cruel fate for the boy to survive only long enough to suffer a more protracted death on land.

"What does he need?" Konrad urged him to try—for him, for Khale, for the boy who thought he would be king.

Ambrose straightened his back like a new fern frond unfurling itself. "Supplies I don't have here." He looked toward the west, toward the village. "I'll need to walk home." He reached into his kit and withdrew a tin box. "Flint, steel, and char cloth," Ambrose told him. "Start a fire. Keep him warm and dry."

Konrad sat up and eased Weston back against the tree. Weston looked at Ambrose. "You know, they don't have fire anymore. Can you outcast a fire fairy?"

They. Konrad stepped a few feet away and breathed in the scent of ocean breeze riding the night air. It would be *we* in time, not *they*. Ambrose, for the convenience of not outraging the majority of the islanders, had set Weston to the same fate as the rest of them.

He took deep, steadying breaths.

Behind him, Ambrose said, "We don't have a fire fairy."

"That sucks," Weston announced. He places his hands behind his head in mimicry of Konrad's own stance. He wondered whether it was deliberate or whether Weston simply did so to open the airway to his lungs.

He decided it was the latter.

Ambrose spoke in a gentler voice, luring Konrad from his anger. "The merchant ship, which departed yesterday, brought your uncle Dorrance."

When Konrad was a boy, Dorrance had been the family curse, the great-uncle who had spoilt the good Selig name in the eyes of other islanders. Konrad was meant to be their redemption, evidence that his grandfather's side of the line was clean of the curse.

Instead, he'd killed his betrothed, on her birthday no less, and ended up banished to the island. By the time he'd arrived on the island, his Uncle Dorrance was gone. He'd obtained a gift from somewhere which enabled him to travel safely.

Dorrance had returned. Either he'd lost the gift, or he wished to visit for one reason or another. Or he intended to pass the necklace along.

He would never give it to Konrad. That much was certain.

Still, from Weston's prediction that Konrad would leave the island...an ember of hope sparked in him.

"Has he still got that necklace?" he asked. He kept his eyes out of sight of Ambrose, lest the man see the hunger that welled in his soul.

"He has," Ambrose confirmed. He nudged the bag with his foot. "Keep the extra fire supplies." He opened a different bag. "Build the fire. I'll assist you in healing him."

Weston needed the warmth of flame and ember. He lay limp against the tree, more still than Konrad liked.

Konrad rejoined him once he'd struck steel to flint and seen the char cloth catch the tinder at the base of his fire. He sat beside him now, intending to sleep in a few moments. He would need his strength for the morning, and Ambrose would be gone for hours.

"You may be right about leaving this island," he told Weston.

In the spring of the year, perhaps, if he could only talk his uncle into choosing to give it to him.

"Told you," Weston coughed. "You won't like how."

"How is that?" Konrad asked. He ought to let the boy rest, but perhaps talking helped him to keep his breathing up.

"Why does he outcast the gay men if he isn't afraid of you?" Weston asked.

Konrad buried his annoyance at Weston's refusal to share how they might leave. It was within his rights, but it called to mind warnings about fortune tellers who would share only enough to entice a person into coming back. Into paying more.

Weston didn't want to be paid, he reminded himself. He must have another reason for not wanting to discuss it.

Konrad quelled his curiosity and answered the question. "Ambrose sneaks us supplies when he can. If he refused to outcast us, they'd elect someone else as leader." No doubt someone who hated them or wanted to kill them outright. He added, "The distinction appeals to the others in the village. It says that they may be banished to this island, but at least they aren't *us*."

"And what makes you better than someone else?" Weston asked. It was an odd question. Konrad had no answer. He was relieved when Weston added, "Why don't you just die?"

It was as if he could read Konrad's own mind.

This was the crux of the problem with the necklace: it could only be worn by one man; it could only free one man from the isle.

"When Khale goes," Konrad said, "I'll die. I won't leave him."

A necklace for one was useless in Konrad's case. Konrad wouldn't use it, and he knew Khale enough to not bother to offer it to him.

"Will you leave me?" Weston asked.

Khale wouldn't. Khale would do anything for Weston.

Konrad wasn't that man.

"The idea is to get you off the island," he reminded Weston.

"Okay," Weston said.

Konrad suspected he was as dissatisfied with that answer as Konrad was with Weston's refusal to follow up on his ominous *you won't like how you leave the island* statement.

He felt badly for Weston, but he reminded himself that he was the one who had snatched the bread out of Weston's hands and stolen from him to give to himself. He wasn't fit to look after the needs of anyone.

11

WESTON

The air was dry on the west side of the island. Weston would have thought it a good thing, except the dry air was punishing in his conditions: his cough choked his body and robbed him of air. Daggers of pain pierced him with every breath as fluid filled every inch of his lungs. His chest rose and fell in rapid, painful bursts and his skin felt like ice. His chest was heavy, a burden he wished he could drop at his feet and move away from.

Waiting for help fell between torture and respite, leaving Weston unsure if he was prepared for what would come next.

His body tensed under the knowledge that he would soon feel better but not be healed yet. The journey to improvement would—eventually—forge the bond between him and Konrad into something unbreakable, by time or distance or any other possible reason.

Beneath the darkness of his eyelids, his hearing was stronger. He listened as various things were set in the soil beside him. Some sounded heavier than others. Most sounded undesirable.

"You'll need these," Ambrose told Konrad. He'd returned, though Weston had missed the exact moment. "He'll need to be upright. I'll hold him for you."

Ambrose pulled Weston's body up, so he would be dangling

toward the ground if he was looking. It was close to flying, he imagined. Just a bit less comfortable.

"You'll need to cut him here," Ambrose said, touching his back.

Weston recoiled. *Cut?* That sounded bad.

"And here," Ambrose continued. "Through the skin and the layer below it, between the barrel bones."

No. What about dying? Dying was the option Weston wanted. Ambrose kept talking about inserting things and what would come out. Things Weston was determined to not be part of.

"You can't do it?" Weston complained.

"Alright, I can," Ambrose said. "Hold him tight."

Weston squirmed, his body's fear overpowering his sense of self-control. Konrad held him tight, forcing the matter.

"Ready?" Ambrose asked.

No, no he was not.

"No," he managed to belt out.

"Tell me about your favorite horse," Konrad insisted.

He didn't have a favorite horse. He had an island surrounded by water he couldn't get to fast enough. Tears stung his eyes, betraying his sense of adulthood. Konrad held him tighter and stuck a stick near his mouth.

Oh, that will help, he thought sarcastically. Weston had the worst sort of luck. He knew exactly what he was about to experience.

"No one makes alcohol here?" Weston asked, trying to stall the inevitable a few more moments while thoughts brewed inside his mind and festered.

"I'm not known for drinking," Ambrose said.

Weston's eyes bugged out and he saw Ambrose laugh and hold up a dark bottle. "I have enough to clean you, not enough for you to drink."

"Use it to clean," Weston decided.

Ambrose kept talking, but most of it had to do with the lack of supplies and hiding what he had taken from others. Instead of listening, Weston tried to think of constellations, naming them and thinking of the legends bound to them.

He began with Qaesius, the star named after a Dragon prince. He was a warrior set on vengeance, filled with rage. He was a lesson to all to not let rage consume your soul.

Tears poured down Weston's face, and his teeth sank into the wood with each second. Not only was it painful, but it was unsanitary.

The blade cut through his skin, slicing through layers of flesh and muscle. Then came the tube. Konrad held him tight, so he couldn't arch away. His screamed beneath clenched teeth, every ounce of scream exploding from his body. Konrad held him tighter, forcing him still as the pipe slid between the edges of his flayed skin, deeper into his body.

A sucking sound consumed Weston's mind as fluid filtered from the pipe, trickling to the ground. He wasn't sure if it had pierced out the other side, except that he hadn't felt a new level of pain as he would expect of a rod ripping through his chest.

Regret flooded through Weston. Why couldn't he have died in the storm?

The pressure inside his chest changed as fluid dripped out. Searing shocks with every tremble echoed down his body, burning his nerves in waves. The pain ebbed into a dull burn that was over-powered by the need to get the tube out of his body. He felt choked by pain, but he could also feel the air flowing into his lungs as the proce-dure progressed.

It was an antagonizing mercy.

"Alright, then?" Ambrose asked.

Weston could breathe again, though he was a mess of tears.

"Yeah," he gurgled through the wooden bit. It would forever have his teeth imprinted. He would be lucky if didn't take a tooth with it.

His body sighed in relief. The pain had crested. With that exhale Ambrose pulled the pipe from his body and poured burning alcohol over the wound. Weston tried to scream, but the wood choked his voice. When the cleansing was over, Weston coughed through the pain, tears staining his cheeks in another episode of their betrayal to his self-proclaimed strength.

"What if it happens again?" Konrad asked.

Ambrose handed Konrad the bloodied supplies, including the bottle of alcohol. "Keep these. I have more." He reached down and removed the bit from Weston's mouth. "You're done now."

Weston felt faint at the sight of the tools that had mauled his body. Luck said they would be needed. He also felt frustrated by how stingy Ambrose had been: He had *more*.

"I'll be heading out," Ambrose said. He stood and brushed his hands off. "Take care."

He patted Weston's shoulder, his fingers squeezing around the top, and glanced at Konrad.

Weston could sense tension; Ambrose hadn't offered Konrad any of the expected exchange; no word of Weston getting off the island.

"You'll regret the necklace," Weston said.

Konrad set to work stitching Weston's back closed. His steady hands did not betray any emotion he might feel. Weston's face, however, betrayed all of it. His face scrunched and contorted beneath the needle pricks.

"I'm not leaving the island," Ambrose replied. "This is my home. I fear the world would imbalance me."

Weston shook his head slowly, so he wouldn't move his back. Konrad had wrapped a piece of fabric around his body to act as a bandage and was just finishing up the knot. The pressure added to the ache.

"Then give the necklace to Konrad," Weston demanded. "Family. It belongs in the family." He knew he was giving too much away, but he couldn't help his desire to fight for Konrad after the man had fought for him.

"No one needs to leave; I intend to burn it," Ambrose said.

"Words fallen on deaf ears," Weston mumbled as he rested his body against the ground, on his stomach to avoid the infection of dirt. Not that he cared at the moment, but he knew he would in the long run.

"It has already created dissent among the men of the village. Imagine if I gave it to him," Ambrose stated.

Weston looked at Konrad, and he felt the death instantly—the uncle that had brought the necklace had been killed in an altercation that night. They would never see Konrad as worthy.

"Yeah," Weston replied.

"You'll learn the way of the place soon enough, and in the spring, we'll send a boat around to collect you and get you home," Ambrose said. He left after those words, cresting the hilltop without another word.

In that silence, Weston knew Ambrose didn't expect him to survive the winter.

Weston lay there while Konrad gathered the supplies in a rucksack to carry over his shoulder. He bustled around then leaned against the tree and looked at the stars.

"I'll leave without you before the spring." Weston tilted his head toward Konrad.

The truth was that the death of his uncle was not the first loss Konrad would experience. Weston wished he wasn't there to bring so much pain to everyone. Too many lives would be lost soon. Was it a coincidence he'd arrived at such an important moment in Konrad's life?

Weston doubted it. The subtleties of Luck were hard to track, but those with it seemed to end up where they belonged when they belonged there.

It was a tricky existence to navigate.

"Without me?" Konrad asked. "What happened to making you a king?"

"It isn't worth the sacrifice," Weston explained. "My part in this—"

"You seem to believe something, such as a changing of the tide, may be coming."

Weston shifted and stared up at the stars. "I believe a tide is here, and I am but a piece of the unfolding puzzle. Hopefully I'm wrong," Weston stated, with an empty conviction and a hunger for life that he knew he couldn't starve. "I hope I die instead," he lied.

"What do you see?" Konrad asked.

"Khale," he admitted.

Silence hung between them, a thousand unspoken words and feelings that passed in the truth that his magic was spot on; there were many paths, but none led to Khale's life and happiness.

"Is it avoidable, within reason?" Konrad asked.

"If I leave without you," Weston lied.

Khale, regardless, was probably doomed in life. A flood, a storm, a plague, a variety of other ailments. Whatever the means, his time was coming to an end. He would have a longer life without Weston in it.

"What would that mean for you?" Konrad asked.

He didn't want to investigate it. It felt wrong, teaming with insanity. "It could be worse," Weston replied.

"In what way?"

"I won't die," Weston said. He would just float out to sea, float back in, and hide somewhere on the island, avoiding others by his intuition.

"Will others, because you are not their king?"

"Probably," Weston replied, defeated. He was asking Ambrose, a stranger, to sacrifice something he loved for him. It was unreasonable.

"Do you know the stars?" he asked Konrad.

"I do," Konrad replied. He pointed to the sky, toward a star that wobbled subtly. "That's the king who returned from the dead and died again. You see the points of his crown?"

"The jagged ones over there?" Weston joked. He lifted his finger in the wrong direction.

Konrad chuckled then took his hand, aligning it with the crown of Qaesius.

"Ah. Yes...I see now. Qaesius. And the box shape next to the points is the home of Maelchor," Weston added to a box that came to a point like a simple pitched roof home.

"You know the stars?" Konrad asked, his eyebrow raised.

"Some of them." He'd wished he knew more.

"Would you like to learn the rest?"

"Yeah," Weston replied. He wanted anything to distract from the subject of their future, of Khale's future.

Konrad leaned back and began telling Weston the stories of each constellation. Weston loved the stars, not just for navigation but because they held the entire culture in their hands—his mother's words.

It was comforting and almost felt like the way he'd always wished home had felt: Safe, warm, and with someone who belonged among the ranks of family.

12

KONRAD

The walk up the mountain toward Ambrose, carrying Weston, had been light.

Now they descended, side-by-side, and Konrad felt heavy.

Heavy with the revelation about Khale.

Heavy with the knowledge that Ambrose wasn't the friend he'd believed him to be.

Heavy with an unsettled weight, like an anvil, which wouldn't name itself or come into the light.

The gifts which Weston possessed were not nearly as appealing as Konrad believed them to be. They were dark and rife with unlucky snares. Nothing was as pure or straightforward as it seemed.

If Konrad's life were a solitary line, it would have run straight and true, parallel to Khale's in nearly every place—until this week. At which point, it would have become a scrambled knot with no apparent outcome.

With Weston's magic dooming Khale, Konrad couldn't help but hope for his own imminent death. He did not believe that was what Weston had in mind for him.

The so-called Luck infuriated him in its ability to predict. He suspected it would not have a similar ability to protect Khale, or Weston would not have brought it up.

He needed Khale like a fish needed water and a man needed air.

When they'd first met, a couple of men had just been sentenced to the Stilts. Konrad knew his preferences by then, and had promised himself he wouldn't yield to any desires he felt for any man. The life in the village wasn't ideal, but it was comfortable and far more varied than Konrad imagined life in the Stilts to be. The village offered schooling, tradesmanship, brotherhood, and a purpose. From what Konrad could tell based on rumors he heard in his youth, the Stilts were essentially a brothel for men who liked men.

It wasn't to Konrad's taste, so he'd vowed to avoid it whatever the cost.

Then Khale had reached the island. He'd been young then at twelve—too young to draw Konrad's interest. He'd grown to adulthood in just a few short years, soft and uncertain and pure. Konrad loved him from afar.

It had begun with a touch—with brushing past each other in the hall. They'd both turned to apologize, Khale's eyes glittering through a gap in his auburn hair. The one encounter turned into other encounters—excuses to brush against each other in the halls and the kitchens, reasons to seek each other's company, until one evening, late and alone in a storeroom, Konrad capitulated to the demands of soul and body.

Their first kiss had been catastrophic, both devastating and perfect.

For months, they concealed their relationship. When they were caught, their trial was perfunctory. Neither of them cared about it; capture was a relief, an opportunity to begin their lives together as a couple.

They'd reached the Stilts, taken in their new lives with shock and resolve, and never once looked back.

Now Weston was here to ruin it, to demand that Konrad and Khale give each other up, that Khale give up any chance at a future, so Weston could do more with his one life than either of them could with their two.

Konrad was willing to die if Khale did. Life without him would be unbearable.

"How long have you lived here?" Weston asked.. The exertion, or the surgery, or some mix of the two had put some color back in the boy's face.

"Just shy of a thousand years," he told him. "I was younger than you are now, when I first arrived." He'd killed someone when he was young.

Perhaps Weston could convince him that this plan, which doomed Khale, was worth the struggle and grief. He doubted he could ever be convinced of that, but he thought Weston should at least have the opportunity to try.

"How long have you lived at the Stilts?" Weston prodded.

Double-banishment. He squared his shoulders, ready to face the beast he would rather not encounter. "When you are king, what will you change in Wyvern?"

"I don't know," Weston said. Konrad liked that he didn't shrug. Another young man—most young men, he thought—would have. "I've never thought about it. It's my family's dream, not mine." He turned to look directly at Konrad, squinting to shield his eyes from the morning sun. "Why didn't you lie to live better?"

Pride. Excitement. The belief that anything, together, would be an improvement on everything, apart. He cleared his throat. He doubted, at this age, that Weston could fully grasp the dedication of new lovers. "A number of reasons," he said instead of the full truth. "For one, we were caught. For another...even had we remained celibate, I think the affection would have been obvious. For another, most of the villagers are unaware of the conditions we face in the Stilts." They had not understood the full price of their affection until they had arrived.

"Do you regret it?"

Did he regret it? Did he regret watching the man he loved wither slowly towards nothing, towards starvation or death in a storm or whatever else happened? Yes, to that.

Did he regret any of his millions of seconds with Khale? Never. Even their worst moments, occasional arguments and desperate hunger were imprinted deep within Konrad. How could he regret himself?

Did he regret now, this young man, these demands? Absolutely.

"I don't regret Khale," he said. Even now, even if he lost Khale, Konrad could never regret loving him, choosing him.

"I don't want him to die because of me," Weston clarified, his words feeling unnecessary to Konrad. No decent person craved the death of another.

"If he dies," Konrad assured him, "it will be because of the nature of this place, not because of any choice you made. The land and the men are harsh."

He dreaded the return to the Stilts. There would be an ugly argument, a moment in which he suspected the characters of some of the other Gancanagh would be laid out for all to see.

Konrad had no place to judge any of them. He'd taken bread from Weston.

"Nivern is harsh," Weston stated. "There are tornadoes and earthquakes all the time. They're under the control of Wyvern, across a strait."

Weston lacked a body that bespoke harsh conditions. The land of Nivern might be harsh, but Weston himself had likely never suffered for it. Or if he had, the suffering was mild.

Perhaps he'd witnessed it among others... "Do they tend to Nivern?"

"Not really. Everyone there hates Wyvern."

He doubted that. Games of power were so layered in light and shadow, avarice and compassion. Hatred was simple; relations between kingdoms, complex.

"If you become king, you'll free them?" he asked. That was a thing he could tell himself: Yes, Khale dies, but thousands regain their freedom. It might let him sleep at night.

"How?" Weston asked, incredulous. He bent over and hacked out a series of delicate coughs, his body arched and his face squinted. Konrad suspected were choreographed to avoid the pain which must sear through his incision site with each movement.

When he stood again, pale with a sheen of new sweat on his forehead, he added, "My dad works for the *kingdom*."

Konrad's mind was either incapable or unwilling to follow the path of Weston's thoughts. "Will you explain?" he asked.

"My dad used our Luck and his knowledge of other magics to gain favor in the houses of Wyvern and Nivern. If my brother marries the princess of Nivern, he thinks we can calm the tensions. Gain power and favor. He favors my brother to rule."

If Nivern had its own princess, why did Wyvern rule over them? It made no logical sense. Why not simply rebel and reclaim their freedom?

"What do you need me for?" Konrad demanded. "I have no skills where women are concerned, certainly not with gaining anyone's favor."

Let him stay here on the island with Khale. There was no purpose for him in the world Weston described.

"I don't want to work for my dad. He wants me dead," Weston said. His voice was careful as though he puzzled his way through the explanation in his mind while he spoke it aloud. "Everyone hates their house for a reason. I would die by one of a dozen attempts for my life. Why would I support something everyone hates? Why would I put myself in his way? My mom made us leave Wyvern for a reason. But I would take Nivern for myself...or I have to stay in hiding."

One thing was certain: regardless of which choices Weston made leaving here, if Khale gave his life for Weston, then Konrad would ensure Weston lived a full and good life. He would make it a worthwhile sacrifice. He would make sure Weston was able to spend his life improving the world by whatever means he could manage.

"You would forge your own path?" he asked. He could see it...Konrad knew dozens of combat styles, weapons use. His only opponent had been Ambrose and occasionally Khale with sticks, something that usually drew the derision of the other men at the Stilts.

The Gancanagh, as part of their banishment, could be called upon to serve the Isles in battle. Because they were disposable men, they were the most obvious choice for the front lines. In the village, swordplay was treated as a sacred trust, to protect the ancient and excellent heritage of the Isles.

In the Stilts, swordplay was banned. If the Gancanagh were ever sent to the front lines, the men of the Stilts were meant to die immediately in battle. It was a term of their banishment from the village. The men looked at sword-fighting with scorn; why protect those who banished us and let us starve?

For Konrad, the question was much simpler: why die if we need not?

He kept himself, and Khale trained whenever he could.

He realized Weston had answered his question, and he hadn't listened.

He needed a new question then, rather than ask the boy to repeat himself. "What about the princess?"

"She doesn't feel right."

Doesn't feel right.

Part of Konrad knew Weston should listen to his feelings. In a way, whatever this magic was, it was all Weston had now.

Part of Konrad didn't care. He imagined a life bound to the whim of Weston's latest instinct, making and perfecting the same plans over and over from different angles, all based on whim.

"You understand," Konrad began. Anger colored his tone, so he strained to lighten it for Weston's sake. What came out sounded choked and desperate. "You're asking me not only to let Khale give his life for this endeavor—which he will do willingly, no doubt—but to go on alone without him."

"Yes," Weston replied. "I am."

He glowered at Weston, demanding *more*. "What good does it serve?"

He watched Weston grapple with the question—a problem most

men wouldn't care to delve into, never mind one so young. "You can't change here," Weston mused. "But there are lots of places we could change." He frowned, sighing back into the cavity of his chest. "But that sounds like a lot of work."

"Change in what way? Help me to see," Konrad all but begged.

In the great scheme of Khale versus the world, the world was losing. Khale was a man Konrad would tear down the world for, and Weston wanted him to tear down Khale for the world. For him. For a young, foreign man with malignant Luck.

He felt the anger building within himself.

"Here, everything is unfair," Weston said. "They're stubborn, and you have no power. What if you could change other places?"

"What would I change?" Konrad lashed out with his voice. "The style of clothes they wear?"

Weston didn't cower under his anger. He straightened his shoulders and met Konrad's eyes with a frustration of his own. "You want food, right? You could make sure there weren't other groups that were starved for useless reasons."

"Do they starve in Nivern?" he asked.

"Yeah, and houses fall down, and no one helps them. No one cares, except that they contribute." Weston scowled, possibly at some memory. But no, it was an intuition. "I don't think we will go to Nivern right away."

Whim again. "Where do we go?"

"There's a kingdom that's falling apart. Worse conditions. We can start with them."

Start with them, as though there would be a line of kingdoms, a string of people to help. Not only the one land but a few. Perhaps a lifetime of lands. Redemption for the guilt, a way to keep his mind off the loss of Khale, a way to spend his time until they could be together again in the world of the dead.

Dead. The word echoed hollow in Konrad's mind, in his heart. Khale's face came unbidden to him: the curve of his jaw, the scent of his skin, the pressure of his lips, the ideas in his eyes, the world of thoughts that was all Khale and only Khale.

To see that gone from the world, all his goodness wasted on this island for nothing...

But then, how many lives such as Khale's were wasted elsewhere?

He worded it carefully. Never would he agree to Khale's death, but perhaps there was some middle ground he could hide himself within. "Alright," he said to Weston. "If the tide of events carries us off the island, I'll help you make change."

Weston stopped walking and looked northward. Konrad braced himself for whatever the boy had to say. "Come this way," Weston urged. He walked a few dozen feet from the path, dropped to the ground just inside the entrance to a shallow cave in the hillside, and began digging at the loose earth.

After a moment, Konrad assisted him.

They cleared away a patch of gravel and damp moss and discovered beneath it something impossible: gold.

Konrad gaped in silent shock.

"Why don't you mine this?" Weston asked.

It wouldn't work. He knew it instantly. If any of the Gancanagh in the village attempted to buy things with gold they shouldn't have, the Selkies would banish the Gancanagh to some further, more hostile breaker island. Some merchant would get the gold, and the Gancanagh would lose everything they'd built.

Perhaps there was something though...Konrad would be happily banished to another island if it meant Khale lived. "Can we use this to save Khale?" he asked Weston

"I doubt it will work," Weston said.

The words slammed into Konrad. Worse than the first time Weston had said it, because this time he said it with such certainty— as though it were fact and not future.

"We could try," Weston added in a softer tone. "Ambrose...don't trust him."

"I'm beginning to discover that for myself," Konrad assured him. There was no reason, save malice, to refuse Weston a place in the village for the winter. He wasn't sure what game Ambrose played, but he was sure that Ambrose meant him, Khale, Weston, all of them in the Stilts, to forever be on the losing end of that game.

"There's something I haven't figured out," Weston stated. He scraped his toe along the gold, leaving a clean, more lustrous strip. "If there are no more shipping vessels this year, how do we get off the island?"

Escaping the island would be the least of their worries. In the winter, the tumultuous sea was unforgiving. Already Weston had been shipwrecked in the volatile currents.

"There are dories for transporting goods from shore to ship and back again."

"And then?" Weston asked.

He smiled. "With luck," he teased, "we have fair weather and calm seas."

"Maybe," Weston said, which meant *no*.

"Or...?" Konrad asked. If Weston had something better in mind, he was happy to hear it.

Weston only shook his head. "I don't know."

Disappointment coursed through Konrad. A moment later, suspicion replaced it. "Someone had a felucca when I first arrived, but Ambrose had it burned."

It wasn't much larger than a dory, but it had a sail and was more seaworthy.

"Ambrose lies a lot," Weston confirmed. "I think he put it in a cave."

He wouldn't be able to move a felucca, in secret, to one of these caves on the mountain. "There must be some caves along the shore," he surmised.

Hope. It was strange but present.

If only they could save Khale too. They would have to. Konrad couldn't foresee a world without Khale in which Konrad could think well enough for him to do the things Weston believed him capable of.

"There are low caves that are drowned out during high tide."

Low tide, then. They would need to watch the moon and plan

their escape according to its movements. "Will it work?" he asked Weston.

Weston set his lips in a straight line. "We need it to," he said.

It wasn't any sort of answer, and as they progressed toward the Stilts, it became more apparent that Weston hovered on the edge of a delirium, his thoughts sometimes coherent and sometimes jumbled and chaotic.

It seemed that draining his lungs had done nothing for the poor soul.

13

WESTON

"They may not be pleased to see you," Konrad said as they descended into the misty harbor. Weston could barely make out the shape of the stilt houses through the heavy air, but he knew they were getting close.

They would be unhappy to see Weston back, with their scant resources. They would have been more pleased if Konrad felt confidence in the mines, but Weston could also feel the tenor of trouble the gold would bring. Still, there was hope. Weston could offer them things, his Luck could make their lives easier. They could learn to appreciate him.

When the individual bodies, moving through the haze, were visible, Konrad put more distance between them. The wind whipped more fiercely, without the shelter their closeness had created.

At the Stilts, they watched the men, splashing in the shallows as they heaved a chest out of the water. The tide kept pulling it back into the sea. Together the men were able to hoist it onto rocks once and for all.

Without a way to heat or dry himself, Weston wondered if he, with his fever and the infection, might be in better shape than them.

In a few hours, the storms would return, and the relentless weather would threaten more of their lives.

There was so little hope, yet the Stilts continued to push themselves to survive their circumstances. It amazed Weston. There was a place for fae at the bottom of every society, but it did not need to be so despairing that even beetles prospered in comparison.

It felt much like home, where his father used people as slaves and servants. Would Weston have woken up to the inequality if he had not been forced from his place of comfort? Shame rippled through him, accompanied by the chills that came with fever.

Weston did not want to be a king who harmed others. He wanted to be a king who tended to his people like a flock of sheep.

His father had studied the magic of all the realms—magic that existed, magic that was theorized. It was part of how he leveraged himself within Wyvern. His uncle had been a fire fae, while his father carried earth in his blood. His experience and knowledge were the two largest tools he used to predict things and gain the trust of the royal house in Nivern—that, and his mother's Luck.

Weston hoped Luck had carried her to safety. He hoped to see her again, someday.

"You really think they *might not* be pleased?" Weston asked. He cocked his lips into a grin, bracing against the ache his gait caused. "Now who's the optimistic one?"

Konrad laughed and continued walking toward the sea, unaware of the deep thoughts brewing in Weston's mind.

They would hate him. They may have thought better if he'd brought something worthwhile. The chests they found were not gifts from him, but products alongside him. He doubted many of them saw him as anything more than a hungry, mouthy, nuisance.

It didn't matter. Weston would find a way out. How, he didn't know yet. The Stilts represented a lesson he would carry with him, through every challenge he faced for the rest of his life. He knew now what his mother wanted from him: to see the world from a new lens, to be free of his father's perspectives, and to want something better. To want others to have better.

His mother, as wonderful as she was, had not been born elite. She was from a lower place in society, one that she'd risen from, then fallen back to.

That fact alone was part of why Weston was in danger from his father: The heir of an undesirable partnership could be outdone by the heir of a desirable one. His half-brother did not carry the Luck he carried.

Their movements were slow. He knew Konrad walked slower for him. Weston felt shame in his desire to survive. He had fought with every breath he had to land on the rocky shores of this place, where deaths would follow his life.

He also wondered if Konrad walked slower because of apprehension. The air between them vibrated with fears of what would come next. The fears grew as more faces looked at them through narrowed eyes, and suddenly, things were real.

Weston's future would cost others their lives. Like the theorized magics his father never found, what they would give their lives for might turn out to be nothing more than a hope. Eyes like these, that would never see him for the change he wanted to create. Eyes that would suffer because he thought there could be more to their lives.

Was it really better to revolt?

Was it even possible?

Weston hoped his psyche would clear with the infection. He was too young to go mad with the hopeless ideas of a Luck prince on the run.

But with fever, there was clarity: There were no other choices. Each path he considered led to the same outcome: Konrad would lose Khale. He could stand up and set forth on a path that could save others, but Khale's fate was inarguable.

Some of the Gancanagh began watching them. Their approach had been noticed, all eyes taking Weston in.

"You know where the knife is?" Konrad asked.

"I'm not diving into your pants, even if my life depends on it," Weston joked. His voice, at least, did not hold the same heaviness of his mind.

He heard air escape as though Konrad wanted to laugh. His tension betrayed his mood. He kept his eyes focused forward, on the faces turning toward them as Weston hobbled through the village. Any sort of modernization, such as gravel paths between homes, was pointless with the tide coming in twice a day. Weston had been lucky to miss the worst of the flooding so far.

Konrad stopped him before they approached the main group. "If you decide to use the knife, you must make certain they don't take it from you."

"I will," Weston replied, unsure of how he would go about it. Someone would need the knife, but he wasn't certain he would be the one to need it. Had he missed a crucial piece of conversation while lost in his mind?

They walked the rest of the distance in silence. Konrad pulled ahead as his home came into sight. When Khale saw them, he immediately headed over to meet them, his movements light the closer he got. He wore an unfamiliar smile that lured Konrad ahead, leaving Weston to watch them reunite. Once he and Konrad embraced, they walked back to Weston.

"How are you feeling?" Khale asked. He looked vibrant, as if he had been filled with life.

"Better."

He could breathe at least, but his skin was coated in sweat.

Khale let go of Konrad's hand. "Good. And Ambrose...?"

Konrad's mouth twitched, almost into a smile. "You have a ward for the winter if you can bear it."

Whatever the cost to Weston, at least it was not Konrad or Khale's doing. None of it was their fault.

Was a *ward for winter* how their fire fae had ended up there for life?

Khale smiled, distracting his line of thought. It was a weird way to accept his fate; for Khale, at least, there was joy in his exile.

Joy...Weston thought about the word. It was the one thing these Gancanagh had, something the others did not. Despite starvation, despite despair, they had each other. They had deep friendships that were built on a need to survive, clearly deep respect even when it lapsed (else they might have eaten one another), and they had love. Every Gancanagh seemed to have a partner, someone to hold at night and share the last bite of food with. Someone to see them through till morning, day after day and year after year.

With nothing else, having each other was enough.

"I think we can manage," Khale said, full of optimism. "Another chest washed up, along with some seeds. They're bringing a third chest in now. If we get Lucky—" he said with a wink toward Weston, "—We can grow a small garden."

There was hope in the chests, but there was also the concern that the more food the Stilts received, the faster they would eat it, and there wouldn't be additional shipments. Luck could only wash so much ashore.

"They're happy, then?" Konrad asked.

He kissed Khale before he could answer, or maybe Weston missed the answer entirely. He set his sights on the ladder. It would be his nemesis for the moment. The first great evil to defeat. In a way, he liked the house. It stood above the water on wooden legs and felt like a home, full of wear and attention. Whatever Khale and Konrad had been in their lives before the island, they were good at building a strong home. It had been built so long ago the wood flooring had worn in the paths they most frequented. Still, the view was incredible. True ocean front property. There was something to be desired about it, amidst the disaster and despair.

The two followed behind him, and they talked about how to get the others in the community to accept him. Occasionally, he felt a hand on his calf, steadying him as he wobbled onward.

At the top, Weston sat on the floor. It was a good floor. He laid back in the beveled groove where they most often walked and let the floor hold him, making sure to tilt his weight away from the incision.

They needed gold. Once they got off the island, they could use it to fund their future.

Weston needed a future to believe in. He had companionship, but he was not used to sustaining his soul on so little.

"Can I just tell them?" Weston asked.

If he helped them, and they were self-sufficient, they would be better off when he left. He could leave on good terms. They'd split the gold. It would be fair.

That was too idealistic: The others would take the gold. Luck and the piece of logic that understood nature and hierarchy agreed it would be unequal, like all things on this island.

"If you'd like, yes," Konrad replied. "But I don't think anything good will come of it." He was in a good mood. His shoulders slouched more, and his eyes were relaxed. Khale did good things to him, things that made Weston doubt existing near Konrad a moment longer.

He could spend the winter in the mountains, hiding and using Luck to avoid confrontation and find food.

Weston wasn't sure what to do. He was tired of wanting to survive, wanting others to survive, and not knowing the best choices for himself and others. It had been days, and these weren't his people. How could he rule an entire kingdom when the pressure was near impossible to bear?

Weston groaned quietly. He was tired of feeling like a philosopher when all he wanted was to eat cakes on the sandy strips of the Angmaan markets. He wanted to adopt tiny animals he would forget about or that his siblings would take from him because they were jealous he got to go on the trip and they didn't.

He wanted to ask his mom why no one else was on the trip and if she had seen this coming. If she hated his dad, or if losing her life with him was worth this. If Luck was a friend you had to make, not a magic you had to learn. How much was his fever and Luck drawing conclusions, and how much of her plots had he discerned from her silence? Maybe she didn't see it coming, but she saw everything coming. He knew there was a purpose. He knew his father wanted him dead.

Would death feel better than this place? Or was this, in fact, Death, and none of them knew it yet.

It was difficult to pinpoint where to direct his energy, except out toward the sea. He listened to the waves as they splashed across the shore. There was opportunity at sea—animals they could hunt, places they could go, and women they could avoid. The men here needed to see the future they could have. Even within their limitations, there was hope.

They had to take the future for themselves. Weston could only feel their way through so many things.

After too long trapped inside his mind, Weston finally replied: "Maybe I will."

"What does that mean?" Konrad asked.

Where Weston had guesses, Konrad was pushy and demanding. He pressed Weston to think of things he would have rather ignored for more pleasant or more focused thoughts—like the shark that was offshore waiting to be caught.

The thoughts he had earlier circled. How could he share his talents without jeopardizing himself and his autonomy?

"It might not make a difference," he told Konrad and Khale. "Here or in the mountains or wherever I go, I may not survive the winter."

Weston wished he could be so carefree again, even for a moment. But had he ever truly been free?

"It might, though?" Konrad asked. He knelt beside Weston and felt his head. "Where has the best chance? Perhaps Luck can be swayed toward survival, if you find the better of the options."

There were many things in the world that Weston believed in: Luck having an opinion about the value of purpose versus happiness, his love for his family, excluding his dad, and the truth that he was sicker than the Stilts could cure.

The hope he'd felt away from the Stilts was gone, as if magic had sapped it from him. Weston tried to move through the feeling, but was there something there? Did a different magic haunt the men of the Stilts?

They, unlike Weston, did not seem to feel hopeless. For him, optimism was a fleeting feeling that he didn't dare touch, not even to rescue Konrad from his own moment of relaxation.

"I don't know," he replied.

14

KONRAD

A s the afternoon wore on, it became apparent that the closed, damp air of the hut did no great service to Weston's breathing troubles, and so Konrad and Khale encouraged him to force himself back down the ladder.

The men had managed to pry open the last of the chests and spread the ingredients along the beach, sorted by use to the men. This chest, unlike the others, held supplies in addition to dried meats. There were beads of such high value that even Konrad's father could not have afforded them. They were spelled by an exotic magic to glow in the darkness and designed to lure fish to a vessel. There were hooks and spools of fine, translucent material. It was easy enough to see how the process worked: tie a bead to the line, sink a baited hook beneath it, and lure the fish with light and the scent of food.

The men would benefit from these tools, if they could manage to use them with care and wisdom.

Konrad sat on the beach alongside Weston and Khale. Khale had his knees drawn to his chest. He drew patterns in the sand beside him. Weston lay sprawled, arms splayed out to drink in the sun.

They stayed like that in relative peace until Urial approached them with a dark expression which brokered no compromise. "What's he doing there?"

Khale shifted his weight so that he sat between Urial and Weston, guarding. "He's living here for winter. The last ship has sailed."

"Not here," Urial argued. "We already don't have enough to eat."

"That second chest can feed us for months," Khale reminded, "if we don't waste it like the first one."

"And then?" Urial demanded. "You think he'll be of any use to us?"

He had already proved of more use than any of the men in the Stilts—Konrad and Khale included. "He leaves in the spring," Konrad promised. "First ship from the harbor." If Weston managed to live that long, Konrad would escort him onto the boat himself to ensure his safe passage off the island, regardless of the price to himself.

"He was supposed to leave yesterday," Goran argued, approaching from the lower beach. "He didn't. Spring is nothing more than a guess."

"He will earn his keep," Khale promised. The wind ruffled his deep orange hair, and Konrad wondered with a sharp intake of breath what it would be to walk these shores without him. To lose him and carry on alone. "With the dolls and the salt mines."

Urial and Goran shared a look. Urial stepped toward Weston, and Khale shifted more.

Against his leg, Konrad felt the cool metal of the knife. He would draw it if necessary to protect an innocent.

"We should kill him now," Urial urged, "before he eats all our food. He's going to die anyway." He stepped still closer to Konrad.

With great care, Konrad made a show to study a sore on his foot, wrapping his hand around the grip of the blade, and sliding it silently from against his leg.

Urial pressed on, "Did you even bring up the dolls?"

It had not come up in the rush to secure Weston's hold on life. Where a man such as Urial placed his priorities on the self and the moment, Konrad was better known for keeping his eye on the future.

Discussing the dolls with Ambrose would have been sensible and true to character.

And yet so great was his concern for Weston that he had forgotten entirely.

"How," Weston croaked, "is murder a reasonable reaction to my presence? I haven't touched *my food*."

"If you eat the food I need," Urial countered, "you're murdering me."

Weston shook his head and pushed himself into a sitting position. He hesitated as though his vision clouded briefly on sitting, and then insisted, "It's my food from the ship."

How in the world was Konrad meant to keep this man alive if he insisted on provoking others? "Weston," Konrad admonished. Some arguments bore value; this did not.

"No," Weston said, stubborn as a mountain. "I have contributed. You," he told Urial, "are just old and opinionated."

Konrad closed his eyes. It seemed Weston preferred a quick death, his neck caught in the vise of Urial's hands, then the protracted death offered by the chest infection.

"Weston," Konrad urged him again. "Please."

To compound matters, Magne approached them, evaluating the situation with his cunning eyes. "What's going on here?"

Death, threats, and worry. Konrad could not decide whether he preferred the quick death for Weston over any death for Khale. None of this was just, but no part of their lives had ever been just. Why should this be any different?

"Weston will be staying through the winter," Khale shared. "And helping with the salt mines."

Magne cast a sympathetic gaze on Weston. A winter here may well be a death sentence for him. All of them knew that, just as they knew a winter here could be a death sentence for any of them. Their numbers always declined most during the winter months, and they lost the most stilt homes in that time as well.

"Sorry, kid," Magne said. His eyes fell on Urial and Goran and urged them to follow him when he left.

"Sorry?" Urial spat. "What are you saying that for?"

"You've seen inside the chests. He's fallen further than any of us," Magne explained. "Would you want to live here, after what he had?"

Urial's shoulders rose and fell in a dismissive motion. "I just offered to fix that for him. Seems they don't like my solution."

Silence hovered between them all as Magne processed this statement. When his mind caught up to the words, he verified, "You just threatened to kill him."

Khale cut in before Urial could deny or confirm Magne's statement. "We don't kill others who show up. He's young, but he's one of us."

"He'll never be one of us," Goran argued, accurately. The men of this community, as divided as they all were by the fight to survive, were united by many things, not least of which was a love of men. All had lost, been outcast more than once in their lives, survived the darkest storms and the highest seas.

"Neither was Gunnar," Weston mumbled.

Goran looked sharply at Weston. "Don't speak of him."

"Mmm," Weston moaned. "But he was family."

If Konrad thought his words would mollify, he might have reminded the men that Weston too had survived high seas and been outcast from those which he loved. Was he not one of them simply by virtue of finding himself on these same shores?

If not, then what made them better than the men who had sent them here?

"He's staying," Khale insisted. He tugged on Weston, encouraging him to stand. Weston groaned his way to his feet and followed Khale's urging arms back toward the ladder, toward the relative safety of the hut.

"Half rations then!" Urial bellowed.

Weston, determined to meet his fate as efficiently as he could manage, called back, "You're volunteering?"

"For all three of you," Goran called back.

Perhaps Khale would die by giving over his rations to Weston. Konrad would have to prevent it, insist that each of them eat their fair third of whatever food they were given or managed to find on their own.

"We'll get our own food," Weston assured them, with the sort of confidence only the young embraced. "We can hunt."

Khale offered his hand when Weston neared the top rung and hoisted Weston the remainder of the way into the hut. Weston grunted as he hit the wood floor and did not rise.

"We'll be fine, Weston," Khale promised. "Magne has significant sway among the others, and Goran is grieving. In a few days, they will settle."

Something about this brought a frown to Weston's eyes, but he said nothing.

"Time," Konrad urged, "without antagonizing them further."

Weston closed his eyes, still sprawled on the floor. The sheen of sweat on his skin had not abated despite the time in fresh air.

Exertion may have been to blame, but Konrad worried something worse lurked under the smooth muscles and bones of his chest. "How are you feeling? The same?"

"I feel fine," Weston said, as if his health were not at the center of every change they had experienced since his arrival. As if he did not matter at all.

Konrad shifted his attention to Khale, to allow Weston time to sleep if he preferred. "If I can conceal the knife from their knowledge, we ought to be able to hunt. Game, even, with practice."

He had experience enough in hunting fish in the shallow water and tidal pools, which formed near shore—using a knife to spear the fish would be easy enough to adapt to. But imagine if he could hunt some of the other wildlife on the island, taste real, fresh meat for the first time in years...

His mouth watered at the thought.

Weston groaned and rolled toward him. "There will be large game in the water soon. We can catch something, cook it, and share it because we have too much..."

"When is soon?" Konrad asked. To share large game, to present it to the other men, and say, *see? We have value for you beyond the menial labor you set us.*

Weston closed his eyes. "Late tonight, when it's dark and the tide is low."

"We'll go then," Konrad decided. What did sleep matter, if losing it meant gaining food, gaining sway among the men. What if the sway could save Khale or Weston?

Khale nodded. He set about rearranging their bedding to make a permanent resting spot for Weston. Konrad assisted him, sifting through the torn and damp materials for the driest and thickest blankets. When they had secured something that ought to suffice, they arranged it in one corner—furthest from their own sleeping area—and carried Weston's sleeping form over onto it, tucking the blankets around him to keep him safe.

When he was settled and asleep, Konrad stole an opportunity to kiss Khale. Since Weston's arrival, they had not had a moment alone. His body was exhausted and hungry in ways he couldn't express. If he must lose Khale, let him share every bit of his love first so that Khale never had any doubts. Let Khale leave this world as loved as when he came into it.

When some time had passed and the breezes coming off the ocean had calmed, Konrad stood. "I'm off for a stick and a vine to fashion a spear from the knife."

From across the room, Weston called, "I'll stay here. Watch the fire."

If Konrad and Khale both left—which they would, to catch and kill whatever was in the water—every man in the Stilts would know Weston was here, alone and vulnerable.

"You can come if you'd like," Konrad offered him. "Help me choose the best supplies."

"I..." Weston hesitated, his focus on something only his mind noticed. He ducked his head as if irrevocably defeated by something. "If you want."

Konrad wanted him safe. Khale wanted him safe, whatever the cost. Konrad wanted Khale safe.

"Rest first," Konrad urged. "We'll leave soon after all of us have slept."

What any of them wanted was irrelevant. The world had its own agenda, potent as the tides, and the desires of three men on one island deep in the sea of one realm among dozens—they mattered for nothing.

Konrad made his best attempt at sleep. The world spun on.

15

WESTON

Weston's mind was clearer, the fit of fever releasing its hold. He still needed near-constant rest. In contrast to his body healing, Weston sensed the opportunity for a hunt growing closer, like a tension building deep inside his chest. He enjoyed that particular part of his magic. He felt the storm brewing in his soul alongside the constant winds that rocked the house. The house was safe, so he allowed himself the chance to enjoy the swaying, like a lullaby sung by his mother.

The lullaby did very little to ease him as a new tension brewed brighter and brighter, pulling at his being and begging for attention.

At last, Weston sat up and watched the flickering glow of fire cast shadows on the walls. He followed the light toward the door. Before him, two men stood. His eyes had yet to adjust to the darkness, but he knew it was Urial and Goran, here to finish what they had started.

"Konrad," Weston whispered.

Konrad groaned and turned toward Khale, his arm falling across Khale's body.

Weston moved toward Konrad, his back aching where the stitches pulled with his movements. Urial and Goran advanced into the room, scanning the space as they inched their way closer.

His hand pressed into Konrad, trying to shake him.

"Leave us alone," Weston demanded. His hands shook Konrad's blanket.

Urial walked across the room. "We're not here to bother you. We're here to help. Get you home. It helps you, and it helps us. Why wouldn't we try?"

Weston's body grew even more tense. It would be nice if they meant the sentiment, but he knew they didn't. Not in a way that was good for Weston's survival.

He could follow them, sacrifice his life for peace and possibly Khale's life, but he didn't want to die. He wasn't ready, and he was selfish.

Regardless of the price that weighed on his conscience, he wanted to live. He wanted to follow the path. He was curious if Luck was right: if there was happiness in his future. But he wasn't sure what that looked like. He wanted to create plans and help others achieve better. He wanted to change the world, or at least a part of it. If he surrendered himself here, to Urial and Goran, he would know.

Weston realized he had chosen his way forward. He would fight for Khale's life, but he knew it may be a self-fulfilling prophecy, with Khale's death ever closer the further he strained from it.

Weston looked at the men. "You're lying."

With his proclamation, they stopped their advance.

"Killing me won't solve your problems. I have skills. I can help you," Weston said, a mix of longing and pleading and hope that they would listen to him with the unsettling finality of their unwavering decision.

Urial's head drew back, the vine twined around his hands, tightening as he stretched it and let a puff of air rumble out of chest, "What skills?"

Weston's heart beat faster, headed toward a gallop. "I can tell you where there are fish. When you'll have inspections. I have a special magic."

Urial shook his head, a wave from side to side as he wrapped the excess vine around his wrists. "You'll have to lie better than that." His feet moved slowly closer, until he could pull Weston out from the nook in the corner. He pushed Weston beside the fire.

Luck said Konrad and Khale were feigning sleep, hoping to gain an opportunity and the upper hand.

While Weston's hand felt the fire pit behind him, Urial grinned. Weston focused on the vines in Urial's hands. He held them outward like he wanted to wrap them around Weston's neck. Goran had the right side closed off, and Khale and Konrad were to his left on their bed. In a split second, Konrad's arm reached along his leg toward the knife tucked beneath his pants. He slid the knife out. Weston dropped to the floor and tried to move between the two men.

Urial pivoted on his heels and lassoed the rope around Weston's neck. He pulled tight, and Weston's neck arched upward, fighting the lengths of the vine as they lacerated his neck. The stitches on his back ached, and deep in his chest he felt a stabbing pain. Urial couldn't have known the wound existed, yet each touch was riddled in agony.

Even if Weston survived, he would have to fight the battle of his wounds again.

He felt the pressure of Goran on his legs as Urial tightened the rope, wrapping it tighter until Weston could not breathe. His head spun in clouds of panic with no oxygen to fuel it.

"Let him go," Konrad barked. The vine pulled tighter against Weston as Urial rammed his body against Konrad's. At the same moment, the weight lifted from his legs, and the pressure around his torso increased. He could hear Konrad trying to fight Goran off.

In another instant, the pull of the vine released, and Weston's head slammed into the wall. He clattered to the floor. Urial slumped on top of him, and blood dripped down Weston's cheeks. Weston breathed, his lungs burning with each breath, until he felt his fingers and toes again.

Finally, Konrad pulled Goran off, and their bodies mixed with Khale's in a tangle of punches and kicks as they moved toward the entrance.

The knife, coated in glimmering red, flickered in front of the hearth.

"Where did you get a knife?" Goran exclaimed, his hand slipping past Konrad's jaw. "You killed him!"

"Where did I get any of our extra supplies?" Konrad asked, his smaller body ducking the blows as best he could. Khale took hold of one of his arms as it swung and pulled it back.

"I have a friend in the village," Konrad said.

Had a friend, Weston thought, his hand still rubbing his raw neck.

"You're sentencing all of us with your actions," Goran warned.

Konrad grabbed the vine and began tying it around Goran's arms and ankles.

Khale tended to Weston; he pulled Urial's limp body off him and gave him both a hand and a piece of cloth to clean his face with.

Khale let his fingers trail above the cuts on Weston's throat. He turned toward Goran. "Grief has overcome you. Think, Goran. You are our brother."

Goran spit on the floor. "So was he."

Konrad turned toward Weston, and his eyes glimmered in the light. "Weston?"

Weston coughed. He felt the blood trickling down his back. He didn't want to deal with the sting of sanitizing alcohol or the chilling sensation of Konrad re-stitching his incision yet.

"Untie his legs and take him with us," Weston replied. There was a shimmer of hope in taking Goran out to fish with them. The largest incentive was extra hands in the water when they caught a shark. It would take their combined strength to wear the beast down.

Konrad kneeled beside Goran.

"Wait," Khale said, his hand on Konrad's shoulder. "Weston's back."

Konrad looked to Weston and then stood. He pulled Weston over toward the table. "Sit," he urged.

He did, though all he wanted to do was run. Across the room, Urial's body glimmered in the flickering light of the fire. All that remained of his soul was a shadow.

Weston looked away at his feet as Konrad lifted his shirt and doused him in the last of the alcohol, before he could flinch away. His back burned, and his eyes raged open. His nails dug into the wood of the chair, leaving a permanent reminder of his pain.

The world felt darker.

Weston tried not to groan as Konrad wove new stitches into his flesh. He failed to withhold the sound, so much so that Khale came and held him steady.

"Why in hell didn't you see this coming?" Konrad asked, the thread pulling his skin tight.

Weston winced. "They came earlier. They hadn't decided when to come back."

"Hadn't they?" Konrad pointed out.

Goran huffed, a grin spread across his bruised and bloodied face.

"I didn't know until they were here," Weston explained. "I was asleep."

"There's nothing we can do to change it," Konrad concluded aloud.

Despite the blood on his hands, it was better this way; the Stilts would stabilize without Urial there, even if it cost Konrad his home.

Konrad was leaving, anyway.

Konrad pressed a bandage against Weston and secured it in place with fabric. "What should we do now, Weston?"

Weston took shallow breaths against the intensified ache. "Take him fishing," he said.

Goran looked at them, his eyes wide. He resisted Konrad's insistence that he stand.

Konrad nudged Goran's foot toward the door of the house. "Down the ladder, please."

"You can't get away with drowning me," Goran said, his voice pitched in panic. He was bartering.

"We aren't killing you," Weston said.

Konrad continued lowering him down the ladder, spitting words up through the light rain that fell, "I did not mean you for you to be part of this," he said to Khale.

"I am part of this," Khale insisted.

The four of them reached the ground and walked in silence into the ocean. The ice-cold water cut through their thin clothes. Weston stayed high enough to avoid the saltwater splashing into his wound. Under a stilts house, Konrad and Khale grabbed the makeshift spear and the vines they had prepared earlier in the day.

Weston yawned. His chest had exploded with pain as air and fluid battled for space. He toppled over from the pressure and pain.

"Are we drowning him?" Konrad whispered.

"No," Weston replied. He trudged deeper into the sea. "He's going to see what I can do, so he stops trying to kill me."

"Good," Konrad replied. He followed, as did Khale. Goran only moved as far as required to not be pushed into the waves. The deeper they got, the more Weston's body buzzed. He would need a new wound dressing if they went much deeper, but even more, there was a risk he would be pulled out to sea forever. He'd survived the ocean once, but would he be lucky a second time?

In the chest-deep water, they waited. Khale and Konrad moved with him, shifting into position so they could trap the incoming beast. Konrad stood closer to Weston, likely to be able to grab him if the ocean threatened to take him. Goran complained until Khale insisted he be silent.

In the desolate space of night, Luck drove every breath. Blood seeped from Weston's back, drawing in the shark.

"It's pitch black," Goran added after a longer spell of silence.

Weston ignored the comment and moved low in the water until he could sense it: the shark was approaching their group, its body twisting through the water with ease as it tracked the blood from his wound.

Weston took the spear Konrad had made and angled it toward the sea. Then, at the exact moment, when Luck said its jaws were widening on approach, he thrust the spear in front of him with every ounce of strength and no regard for the pain that seared through his body.

The stitches broke open yet again, the blood driving the shark into a frenzy.

The shark's mass collided with him, but the jaws fell shy of encompassing his flesh thanks to the netting and the spear's strike.

Tonight, for the rest of the night, Weston would not blame Luck for being a burden in his life. They would feast. The shark would be an offering for the loss of Urial's life.

Weston glanced at Khale and Konrad. "I got it!" he exclaimed.

"Weston!" Khale screeched.

Weston turned in time to see another shark lunging toward him. He toppled backward into Konrad's arms as Khale drove his spear through its head, to cut the animal off. Khale and Goran wrestled the beast, spearing it repeatedly until it took its last breaths, and its body sighed into the worn expanse of death, floating beside the other.

"We have to get you out of the water," Konrad said. Konrad led him out, pulling one of the sharks with him. He looked back at Khale and Goran. "Quick. There will be more. He's bleeding into the water."

Khale shoved the shark toward Goran. "I'll watch our backs."

Goran grunted as he grabbed the tail and followed Konrad.

Despite exhaustion and pain, Weston was filled with pride in the hunt. He carried a fin toward the shore as the men helped the two dead sharks glide through the shallows.

"Do you understand now?" Khale asked. "He will help us."

"Yes," Goran replied.

"Will you stop trying to kill him?" Khale asked.

"I will, but you have to answer for Urial." Goran stared at Konrad when he stated that.

Weston wondered what would come of it. It was a mistake to wonder because, as usual, in his wondering came the answers he wasn't ready for: Konrad and Khale would have to leave the area, by choice or force. Weston would be held prisoner and used for his Luck.

Weston tripped, his mind lost elsewhere, and his face sank beneath a wave. The salt burned his already struggling lungs with the fresh vigor of a future Weston knew he would live to see. Konrad lifted him up, giving the shark he carried to Khale now that they were almost out of the water.

"Come on," he urged Weston. Together, they made it to shore where Weston could finally collapse on the beach, face down to keep sand from his wound.

On shore, Konrad looked at Goran. "I'll answer for Urial in the morning."

Goran looked at the sharks and the three of them. He shook his head then left without another word. Weston watched as he walked up the shoreline to his home. Its support poles were succumbing to the tide.

If Weston had an ounce of trust for Goran, he would have asked him to stay and be around others. He'd lost his partner and was grieving. If they could prepare the meat together, Konrad and Khale could spend time in private. They could enjoy one of their last days together.

As it stood, Weston did not trust Goran, and so he let him go. Weston turned toward Konrad and Khale, "We should start cooking the meat tonight."

If they did, they could take some of it with them when they left. The timing of their departure wasn't clear to Weston, but the sooner the meat was prepared, the better.

"Do you know how to cook this?" Khale asked.

"I can guess," Weston replied. He sat down next to the shark and looked into its eyes. They were hollow and gray, which seemed more like a typical shark than a dead one, and yet this one...this shark was gone. This life had been taken. Weston wasn't one for hunting, but he knew to honor the life taken: he closed his eyes and thanked Maelchor for the day and the food.

"Do you think we should build a smoke box to cure the meat?" Khale asked Konrad. "Fennery's father was a butcher."

"There's enough spare wood," Konrad replied.

"I'll get him," Khale said. He set the vines he had carried in with the shark down and walked off into the night toward another of the houses on stilts.

Konrad and Weston both watched him for a moment. Then, Konrad turned to the shark and began preparing it.

Weston enjoyed the silence of working beside Konrad, aside from the coughing fits and wincing in pain. He saw the glances Konrad made with each fit, the way his hand almost rose to see if Weston's fever had returned, and the way he focused on his work too closely.

"Thank you for believing in me," Weston said. "And for saving me."

"Is he still going to die?" Konrad asked, without looking up.

Weston played out a thousand scenarios as they worked, looking for a detail he could latch onto and give Konrad hope.

"Probably," he settled on. "I feel an ending, impenetrable by any shift in path. I'm sorry. I can still go, but I don't think it changes his fate. I have made a mess of your lives."

"He dies for the murder, but I don't?"

"They won't kill us. I don't know what happens, but it is about the necklace and Ambrose."

No matter what, it seemed to come down to Ambrose and how he responded to the three of them. Weston didn't know how to get a better answer or what to say to Konrad that could comfort him in the unknown. It was the hardest part of Luck: to know but not to know how.

"Alright," Konrad replied, breaking the thought. "Then we stay away from the village. I have no desire to visit there anyway."

A shimmer of hope flashed through Weston's mind: if Konrad were to relax and stop trying to save Khale, Khale may live.

To tell him would only secure his fate. Weston nodded instead. His meddling with Luck seemed to draw them closer to the outcome he wished to avoid.

"You should let me go on my own," Weston said.

"To the village? Are you well enough?"

Weston meant away from the island. He felt a mix of foreboding and prophecy when he thought of Konrad leaving the island with him. The village would be a stop on the way off the island; if Konrad never visited the village, it was unlikely that he would gain access to the talisman that Ambrose was withholding from him. Without the talisman, he couldn't leave the island.

"If it comes up," Weston replied, choosing his words carefully. "I can make it."

"And home again if necessary?"

Weston looked at the houses that comprised the Stilts. Home was a place you belonged. Weston didn't belong here, in these houses. His eyes fixed themselves back on Konrad, on the family he and Khale represented. The Stilts were becoming home to Weston, despite everything they lacked.

"This will go a long way," he replied. "It will last half of the winter if they savor it, balance it with the grains. I can catch more if they let us stay long enough."

Konrad slid his knife across the length of the shark, a large swath of meat falling loose. "Your habit of avoiding answers is very convenient for you, isn't it?"

"Do you want to know the answers? Weston asked.

"Did I ask the question?"

"This won't be home. I won't have something to come back to," Weston stated.

Saying things like *you're my home, and I know I'll find you* felt wildly was pathetic and too sensitive for Weston to face. He needed a better way to phrase it—like *I'll find you because I know you have a knife.*

The complex weaving of ties was something Weston was going to have to work on understanding more; even at the Stilts he could feel the closeness of Goran and Urial that had only forged with Weston's arrival.

Konrad was looking at him. He must have spoken. Weston caught his eyes, the flecks of color that made them Gancanagh.

"Why is that?" Konrad said.

Weston had lost his family in the shipwreck. It was hard to put into words something as factual as someone losing their family when the pain of it was still fresh. He had managed to ignore his emotions on the matter.

"They will probably burn the house and kick us out. They were going to burn it before."

Konrad continued to look at Weston expectantly.

"I think we end up walking around," Weston said.

"There's nothing to be done for Khale?"

It was infuriating to Weston to have such a strong feeling and to have no variable that could be changed to avoid it. He continued to try, again and again, but it was to no avail. No scenario seemed to result in Khale's life.

"Every time I try to avoid it, it feels more certain," Weston lied.

Konrad continued to work on the shark, deboning the meat as he worked along the length of it. He set the bones in a pile on the side.

"I'm sorry," Weston said. "That I'm here changing your life."

He looked down at his hands, useless tools compared to Konrad's. He would learn, but he needed a mentor.

"You're going to be happy someday. I can see the potential," he told Konrad.

He could if he stretched his mind far into the future. He felt the waves of contentment lingering in the far-off future. Even the smallest tendrils of hope had helped Weston survive. He hoped they would help Konrad.

They didn't. Konrad's chest puffed, and he glared at Weston. "And Khale? What will he be someday? What has he known besides suffering?"

The someday part caught Weston in a flicker of frustration. He didn't know how to sort it out or what to even sort, so he settled with, "Maybe, someday, he'll have more."

"You talk in riddles," Konrad accused.

"I don't understand it!" Weston replied. "You try having Luck, and make sense of it! I can see a future where he's a dad. I don't know how dead people become dads, but it's out there in the realm of maybe."

Konrad didn't respond to his outburst. Instead, he focused on the shark. Piece by piece he worked the animal without regard for Weston. He didn't flinch when Weston coughed. He didn't look up as Weston fell to the ground to rest.

It was one of those desirable skills that Weston knew was useful, but made Konrad seem heartless at the moment.

"I won't avoid your questions anymore," Weston said, his eyes flickering shut. "But you have to trust I am telling you as much as I can."

Konrad grunted and kept working.

16

KONRAD

There was no denying what sort of man Konrad was. One death at his hands, as a result of the Gancanagh curse, could not be helped. A second death at his hands marked him as a particular sort of man. It distinguished him from the other Gancanagh.

Worse still was that Urial's lover had died nearly a decade ago. No one would mourn his passing in the way he deserved. The loneliness, the cold tide of winters in solitude, had calloused him, but Konrad could still remember the man Urial had been before Niall's death, the man who chose to help him and Khale when they first reached the Stilts, the man who organized and taught skills the villagers didn't know enough about to punish.

Konrad had repaid Niall's generosity by killing his love.

Perhaps Urial had wanted it.

The bitter taste of Khale's possible death made this an easy avenue to explore. Konrad would find a way to die when Khale did, unless Weston forced otherwise.

But ten years had passed since Niall's death, and Urial hadn't chosen death before now. He'd argued in favor of his own life yesterday.

No, this death was one hundred percent the fault of Konrad. With the knife came the opportunity to use the knife, and he'd proved he could not be trusted with a deadly weapon.

Or he'd proved that he had the necessary skills to protect Weston, and perhaps even Khale.

He knelt on the beach, beside Urial's body, in silent prayer. When the sun rose, he moved away and leaned against one of the poles that held up his house, waiting. The reaction could be bad. It could be the end of his own life.

Casek approached first. He liked to wake at the end of high tide and walk the beach in search of anything that may be useful or edible. Today his walk brought him back to the Stilts via Konrad and Khale's home—or the ground beneath it anyway.

He peered at Urial's body. "He's dead," Casek commented.

"Yes."

Konrad tried to think of something else to say. He wouldn't implicate Goran unless the man chose to involve himself. At this point, it could be put down to a fight between Konrad and Urial, and Khale could be safe.

"He attacked Weston, and we fought," Konrad explained. He pointed a few feet from Urial's body up the beach where they'd lain out the bodies of the sharks in the predawn hour. "We caught them last night. A month's worth of meat. Perhaps more."

Casek glanced back toward Urial's body and then walked past the sharks and ascended the ladder to his own house.

Konrad rubbed the hilt of the knife with the heel of his thumb.

In another moment, Weston approached. "He's not a problem," he told Konrad. "But Goran isn't settled."

Goran, who'd tried to kill Weston.

Konrad broiled at the realization that the men of the Stilts would not be angry with anyone who killed Weston; they would see it as understandable. Weston was *them* where Urial was *us*.

"Who's the problem?" he asked. "Just Goran? Others?"

He was coming to rely on Weston too much over his own intuition. Of course, Goran wouldn't be the only one angry. Magne would be because he'd stood up for Konrad and Khale yesterday. Others in the Stilts would be as well. Anyone who had agreed with Urial last night and had the decency not to act.

"Magne," Weston agreed. "And someone I don't know. Waves of anger. It's hard to tell."

Konrad bit back frustration at Weston's imprecision.

Khale arrived then. In the tiredest of the old stilt houses, he'd been hanging shark meat to cure. Konrad guessed he must intend to use the building as a smokehouse. Now, Khale sloshed toward Konrad and kissed him.

He didn't taste hungry today. Today, he tasted of salt and work.

"How is everything?" Khale asked.

"We're waiting for consequences." Konrad gestured toward Magne and Casek's house. He drew Khale to his side, unwilling to lose any more of whatever remained of their time together.

"You should rest for a few hours," Khale urged him.

Not a chance. "I'm alright," he insisted. "I wish Goran hadn't tackled me."

He kept playing and replaying in his mind the moment the knife had pressed into Urial's neck.

The irrevocability of that instant, the way a single action could cascade into disaster, the fact of Urial's life wiped from existence by Konrad's hand...

He was not alright.

Khale hugged him. "I do too. I love you." He looked at him and ran his fingers through his hair. "Please rest?"

He couldn't bear the thought that he might lose precious Khale time to sleep. If Weston was correct, he had a lifetime to sleep.

"I prefer to be with you for now," he told Khale. He drank in his warmth, his presence, his softness. "I'll rest tonight," he promised.

Magne climbed down the ladder without Casek. "What happened?" he asked. He looked at Konrad in a way that said he had suspicions about what happened, but he wanted to hear Konrad's version before he made up his mind.

Recalling Weston's advice, Konrad let Khale speak: "Urial and Goran attacked Weston last night. We were able to calm Goran down, but Urial wouldn't listen. He had a vine wrapped around Weston's neck."

And with that, Goran became involved.

Konrad sighed.

Magne pointed to Urial's neck, the gaping wound. "Who has a knife?" he asked.

"I do," Weston lied. "I did. Konrad has it now."

"You killed him?" Magne verified.

They might kill him. Better Konrad than Khale. "I did," Konrad admitted.

Magne sighed, eyes on Urial. "What was the point of trying to calm everyone down if you were going to go and do this?"

The way he asked made it even more likely that he suspected this had been a preemptive strike on Urial. He needed to clear this up before it escalated into a spoken accusation. "It was unintentional. I meant to surprise him and lost my footing." Again, he left Goran out. He hoped the man wouldn't be immediately defensive once Magne asked him for his version of events.

"How do I know he attacked you?" Magne accused. So much for avoiding the allegation. "How do I know this wasn't pre-emptive?"

Goran materialized from somewhere, calmer than Konrad expected. "Urial went to apologize," he explained to Magne, calm and serious. "We think Weston should stay. He," Goran pointed toward Konrad, "didn't give us a chance."

"That's a lie," Khale asserted.

It was pointless.

Weston's slumped shoulders agreed with him.

"You attacked him!" Goran snapped. "How would you know?"

Magne drew a long breath and studied all of them in silence. Konrad felt Khale's tenuous hold on the group failing as Magne stepped forward to claim it.

Just so long as Magne never saw the need to punish Khale for Konrad's actions, it would be alright.

"It's impossible to know which of you is telling the truth," Magne mused. He met Goran's eyes. "What made you change your mind?"

"He has magic," Goran said.

That, at least, was no lie. The timing of the revelation would no doubt be misrepresented to paint Goran and Urial in a beneficial light.

Goran explained, "Look at the food that's washed up. He's alive. They found a shark in minutes. No one was hurt killing it."

"We found the shark after the attack," Konrad countered to Magne. "It was an attempt to convince Goran not to hurt Weston."

"It was an example," Goran argued. "The salt mines are another."

Konrad wasn't sure what was meant by that statement. His eyes were on Weston, whose eyes were on the sand at his feet.

Konrad hadn't noticed Casek's approach, but now the man said to Magne, "It doesn't matter why—murder is murder."

"A defense killing is not a murder," Konrad countered. "Weston cannot defend himself while still injured."

Magne was silent a moment. Khale squeezed Konrad's hand.

"If he has an all-knowing magic," Magne asked, "why didn't he just avoid it?"

That marked the end of the productive discussion. The group would wend its way around to the conclusion that Konrad—and probably Khale—had attacked Urial.

"I didn't know they were coming," Weston defended.

Goran laughed in a derisive tone. "You mean we weren't hostile; you weren't expecting friends to come by. You were looking for violence." He turned toward Magne. "That's proof that Urial was murdered."

"Look at my neck!" Weston couched as he tilted his head, showing the vine marks that had cut into his flesh.

"If you had the magic you claim to have, and allowed this to happen, then it was a premeditated murder." Magne rubbed his hand over his beard. It was still short and had only a couple of months of growth to it. He said to Weston in a gentle tone, "Do you have the magic he says you have?"

Without hesitation, Weston responded, "I have earth magic and a strong intuition."

Magne blinked.

He looked at Khale, rather than Weston or Goran, and Konrad's stomach sank. It was one thing to ask Weston to lie effectively. Khale was more transparent, though he tried. He always tried.

"I think," Magne told everyone. He wouldn't meet Konrad's eyes. "I think the fact that he didn't avoid it is proof." He stepped away from everyone, toward the central fire. "We'll need to talk, all of us," he said, and then he walked off, his feet slogging through the soggy sand.

Konrad ran his hands through his hair in frustration as he watched the remaining men follow Magne across the beach.

He cast his gaze on Khale's concerned countenance... "Whatever happens," he pleaded, once they were alone, "leave yourself out of it. I'll say you were sleeping."

Khale looked at him, steady. Konrad had no idea how he remained so calm. Konrad's entire essence was a coil of tension, and Khale was a warm smile. "We'll find a way to smooth this over," he assured Konrad.

"Perhaps," Konrad said for the sake of it. His heart struggled to agree with his words, especially given Weston's defeated expression.

"I'm bad luck," Weston muttered. "Maybe Maelchor is mad at me."

Konrad didn't suppose it would help for him to tell Weston he doubted a god like Maelchor had time to notice, never mind be angry at one young man.

Still, he asked skeptically, "At you?" Even if gods took the time to notice mortals, Konrad doubted Weston had ever done anything to earn Maelchor's ire.

"Yeah," Weston said, exasperated. "You were fine before I washed up."

"Your journey had already begun," Konrad countered. He wasn't sure what point he made, only that he hoped to improve Weston's mood.

"Are we joining the talks?" Khale asked.

"Are we?" Konrad asked him. He misliked the idea of Khale being anywhere near people who decided fates or cast judgment.

"I think we should be there," Khale stated.

"I'll be at your house," Weston told them. "I cause problems at meetings."

If that were the case, Konrad ought to be the one who stayed home.

He wanted to be where Khale was, and Khale wanted to be at the meeting. "Alright," he told Weston. He watched Weston ascend the ladder into their house.

It was strange, the idea of Weston as an adopted son of sorts, even if he was already an adult. Khale seemed to like it, even if Konrad was less certain how to feel about Weston. Konrad watched Khale's eyes follow Weston up the rope ladder, full of concern that he might slip during one of his coughing fits.

He would need another surgery at this rate.

Konrad shouldn't have allowed him to be out all night hunting sharks. It had done nothing to protect them against judgment for Urial. He had no way to prevent the other men of the Stilts from killing Khale if they concluded execution was a fair punishment for Urial's death.

He pulled Khale into a hug. "We can walk away before that meeting and forge our own path," he suggested. "Weston would help us."

With Weston's help, they could likely hide in the mountains indefinitely.

"Walk away?" Khale asked. "Where?"

"Elsewhere," Konrad said with a vague and dismissive wave. "On our own."

"I think we should."

It amazed Konrad how decisive Khale could be at times when he was so unsure at other times. It relieved Konrad that he didn't have to argue Khale into safety; Khale wanted what Konrad wanted. "As do I," Konrad agreed. "Let's go."

He climbed the ladder to their house just behind Khale, deliberately aligning their bodies as much as possible as they made their way up. He loved touch, any kind of touch. Konrad would never have enough of Khale.

"Change of..." Konrad began as they pulled themselves to floor level in their house. He broke off in surprise at the sight of the three blankets full of belongings and tied off.

"Plans?" Weston quipped.

Beside Konrad, Khale laughed, deep and bright like afternoon sunlight on a clear day.

"I didn't mean to touch all of your things," Weston apologized, "but I thought you wouldn't mind because it saves time."

Konrad nodded. He ran his thumb over the hilt of his knife and surveyed Weston's pale skin. He may end up carrying him again. "The faster we leave, the better, I think," Konrad agreed. "Which direction?"

"That way," Weston pointed. "Around the edge of the island. The caves."

The caves, so full of gold. It was a gradual ascent, but Konrad wasn't sure Weston could make it on his own. His coughing fits were becoming shallower—a sure sign that he suffered with pain each time he coughed.

Konrad retrieved the remaining medical items Ambrose had given him. He hesitated by his bed, his hand on the flint set Ambrose had given them.

He decided to leave it. It would better serve the highest number of people when they found it if he left it behind for them to notice and use.

"Should we try and carry fire, or make new fire later?" Weston asked.

He wouldn't be asking if he had no opinion or intuition on the matter.

"Why don't you tell us?" Konrad prodded.

"We should try to bring it with us," Weston decided.

Khale picked up two of the blankets, his and Weston's. Konrad slung his over his shoulder and pulled a longer stick from the fire. "Let's go," he said.

They did, leaving behind the Stilts and a thousand years of memories; carrying with them Khale's life.

With any luck, that crisis was over.

17

WESTON

The three men walked up the winding hills and into the more dense trees. The cliff sides were too dangerous to traverse, but they stayed close to them and off known paths. Weston led the way, using his feelings to navigate them back towards the cave with the gold.

They were on a small island, and Weston knew it was only a matter of time before someone found them wandering outside of the Stilts. If they could collect some gold and store it along the coast, they could retrieve it when they escaped. The path also gave them the option to jump off the cliffs into the ocean. There were even odds they would survive such a jump.

Weston's head was burning, and his ability to predict the future felt more clouded than ever. His intuition was beginning to mix with fire and fluid and the dread of the upcoming surgery he would need.

The surgery was coming too soon. His mind had become fixated on the pain. He kept trying to pinpoint when and how he would have the procedure done. Who would do it, if not Ambrose?

He also tried to focus on staying awake. He was too tired to be hiking through the mountains with baggage.

"These are decent caves," Konrad said. He stepped beyond the threshold, where the soil changed from damp to dry and sheltered. "Does the village know of them?"

Weston shook his head. "They don't care about them. They're too far from the village, and they're on the stormy side. They don't know about the gold."

Khale glanced at Konrad. "Gold?"

"We found it earlier on the walk back," Weston explained.

Konrad moved closer to Khale, his arm across Khale's shoulder, and walked deeper into the cave. He turned back. "Do they flood?"

Weston bit his tongue and thought about the worst storm that could come through: the storm the previous night, rain, whatever he could muster to imagine heavy rainfall. Then, he let his mind wonder if the caves were dry, flooded, or what state they might be in. It was tedious and frustrating to draw on Luck. If intuition was a muscle, he had gone from skimpy to strained over the past few days and it was becoming easier to sift through the possibilities and sort which feelings belonged where. He thought they might be becoming friends, if that sort of relationship could exist with magic.

"No, they're high enough to drain well. We will be safe here tonight," Weston concluded. He didn't just mean safe from the possibility of flooding; he could sense the night wasting away into empty hours of the three of them alone.

Konrad set the bags down—as did Khale—and Weston pulled some shark out from his own stores. "I brought food."

Konrad lit a fire with some of the nearby branches he found and the flame they had carried. They sat near the opening of the cave on the dusty earth and stones, shielded from both the village and the Stilts.

"They would have killed us and kept you prisoner?" Konrad asked.

It was curious that Konrad had waited all hike to ask this question, and there was a sense of their earlier conversation laden in the sentiment. Konrad would not ask a question he was not prepared to hear the answer to, and Weston would keep up his end and be honest and forward with his answers. Most of them, at least. Khale's chance at living depended on Weston's omissions.

"No," he replied. "They were going to kick you out and not let me go along. This way is easier."

Khale laughed, his stick hovering over the fire bobbing with him.

"They'll be looking for you." Konrad stated.

Weston wasn't sure if it was a question, a statement, or a bit of both.

He answered it like a question: "No, they'll give up. It isn't worth it to get caught by the other side."

Konrad nodded and rested his head back against Khale's thigh. Weston shifted to give them some privacy. It was an ongoing instinct with them; they needed time to themselves. He refused to add *selfish during Khale's last days* to his list of transgressions against Konrad.

"We'll need to forage tomorrow," Khale said.

"Some gourds are growing nearby," Weston pointed out.

"Wild grapes grow all over the mountainside too," Konrad's voice echoed down the cave. "And I have the knife. We may be able to set a trap for more meat."

"We will survive," Khale's voice murmured, low and comforting. He began humming a song for Konrad.

Though it wasn't for Weston, it was comforting nonetheless. The soothing tones reminded him he had something here on the island.

Weston rested his head on one of the bags. Somewhere out there was his mom's body, alive or not. He let his mind reach out toward her for the first time. She was alive, Luck promised, but on another island. She was content for the moment, going through her own journey. He would not see her for a very long time.

He didn't want to lose her. He wasn't ready to lose her, even if he was 17. He wanted to see her, not just in his mind but in flesh, one more time.

Someday, maybe. It wasn't a comforting thought.

He refocused his mind on his chest. He wouldn't be able to swim from the island. For one, he would attract sharks. For another, he was too weak. He had fixated so hard on the idea that they would get off the island without an understanding of how that would transpire.

There weren't many options with the frequency of storms.

Somehow, Luck promised they would get off the island.

"We should build a boat," he mused aloud.

"We should build a blind first. This fire? High on the mountain like this?" Konrad said.

"How do you do that?" Weston asked. He watched some bugs crawling across the ceiling of the cave, one getting caught in the sticky webbing of a spider.

All felt important: the bugs, the cave, Konrad, the blind...

"Do what?"

"Build a blind."

"You need rest," Khale urged.

Weston exhaled slowly. "Rest is for the dying."

Khale put his hand softly on Weston's shoulder. "I hate to be the one to tell you, but you're not thriving, Weston."

Weston closed his eyes. "Alright," he mused.

Khale chuckled. "Rest, perhaps, with sleep, you will feel stronger."

"Perhaps," Weston mumbled. He wanted Khale to have that hope, even if Weston knew he would not wake healed. While he fought against worries of his mortality, his mind drifted back to his mom on some rocky shore. She had a boat, but she wasn't leaving. She was there, staying there. He wanted to know why.

"Tree branches crossed over one another," Konrad began. "Placed in the entrance to block light."

"We'll build the blind," Khale whispered.

Khale knew, Weston realized, that their behavior was off or that the way they were speaking was off. Something.

"If I must," Konrad said.

"We'll be quick," Khale assured him.

Weston blinked awake and tried to sit up, his back burning in protest. He coughed hard, a fit that filled his chest with agony. *Now?*

They watched Weston as he pulled himself to standing.

"You have high odds of being fine," he told Konrad.

His hand followed the edge of the cave to stabilize himself as he approached the entrance.

"Go. Let me grow my beard in peace," Konrad said.

Khale laughed and let Weston hold on to his arm as they left the cave.

They moved deeper into the woods. Khale seemed to have his own intuition driving them, and Weston was happy to let him lead. After they'd gone further than Luck felt necessary, Khale stopped, a vine of grapes sprawled before him.

"You're not good at keeping secrets," he told Weston.

Weston tried to squish a grape between his fingers before he ate it. "About what?"

"What happens to me?" Khale asked.

He fixated his eyes on the stars; Konrad must have told Khale the same stories he'd shared with Weston, over the years they had been together.

"I don't know," Weston admitted. "Some people want to kill you. Some people want to kill him. Sometimes I think we manage to make it off the island, but you'll die later. It's unclear."

"Everyone dies, Weston."

"Not everyone dies in the span of my thoughts," Weston pointed out.

"Will you keep him busy?" Khale asked. "You can be needy. He likes projects."

Weston chuckled, despite the pain. "I will."

"Do you know if Ketty forgives me?" he asked.

Weston scrunched his face, trying to pinpoint who Ketty was.

It settled into place: Ketty was his daughter. She had been killed, for what Weston didn't know.

"Ketty forgives you."

Khale cringed. "And her mom?"

Weston took a deep breath and swallowed. "Yes. Her mom too."

They sat together, with grapes and stars and worries of the future, while Weston wondered what Khale's would be. Nothing came of his musing; Luck had no more opinions.

18

KONRAD

Konrad didn't wake until morning. Hours, countless precious moments of time with Khale, were lost.

Nevertheless, he sat in the cave for a moment, absorbing their situation. It was the first real solitude he'd managed since Weston's arrival, and he found he needed the solace of his own mind, the silence which had historically yielded his most useful thoughts.

He had nothing. There was no arguing against the strength of Weston's conviction, the resignation and frustration in the boy's tone when he spoke of Khale's fate. No thought of Konrad's could make a case in favor of Khale's survival—save his own desperation and determination.

He was one man against the tide.

One man, plus Weston. He was more valuable than Konrad, in the matter of saving Khale. If anyone could do it, it was him, not Konrad.

These were the thoughts that drew him out of the cave and into the mid-morning sunlight. From the hilltop vantage beyond the blind Khale and Weston had built, the Stilts were visible in the distance:

square blocks of structure against the silver background of wet sand. Low tide.

If they were down there now, they'd be scavenging.

Instead, he found them in the woods. Khale's shirt was off and he'd fashioned it into a sack to fill with gourds.

"Want some shark?" Weston offered, once they'd noticed Konrad. He unfolded the foil, which had wrapped Weston's bread that first morning and passed a chunk of smoked shark flesh to Konrad.

"Thank you," he said. He found himself drawn to Khale's side, so that was where he stood. "Did I miss anything?" he asked them.

"We made the blind and cooked and talked," Weston said.

"And slept, it seemed."

"You didn't," Khale added. He brushed his fingers down Konrad's cheek, amused. Something in his tone made Konrad wonder what they'd talked about without him there—whether Khale knew of Weston's intuitions about him.

The thought made him want to fix it even more, impossible though it was. "Did it work?" he teased Khale. "Has my beard grown?"

He laughed. "It looks like it has." He reached and pretended to measure Konrad's beard with the width of his palm and then moved his hand down Konrad's neck and onto his shoulder.

If Weston weren't here, Konrad would have pulled Khale against him and tasted his lips and his body and worn away the hours of the morning in his arms.

However, Weston *was* here, so Konrad could only put his hand on Khale's waist and force himself not to exhibit his frustration in a way that would burden the boy. He had enough guilt; he didn't need Konrad's ire on top of it.

Weston looked away and swallowed. When he looked back, he said with determined optimism. "Khale said you can sing well."

Konrad scowled at Khale, amused, and Khale's eyes lit in chal-lenge and mirrored amusement.

A shock of despair forced Konrad to look away.

"He has misled you, I'm afraid," he told Weston. "Khale has a much better voice." He focused carefully on the shape of the sounds his words produced and on the perfect inflection. It was easier to stomach than the other thoughts which threatened to overtake him.

"You'll cave," Weston joked. He set off a few feet ahead of them, walking through the woods toward the cave where they'd slept.

When Weston's back faced them, Konrad sneaked a kiss to Khale. It blossomed for a moment; they'd never experienced an enforced separation, not in centuries anyway, and it made their exchange more powerful than usual.

Khale pulled away and slipped his hand into Konrad's, his narrow artisan fingers swallowed by Konrad's beefier hands. "It's nice up here," he observed to Konrad, "without the water sloshing at our feet."

Konrad agreed. "The dry air should be better for Weston's lungs as well." He called ahead of them to Weston: "How are you feeling?"

"I'm surviving," Weston replied. Konrad wondered whether that was a promise for the future or whether it was only a guarantee for the moment.

"He's been coughing more," Khale answered his unspoken question.

Konrad frowned at the woods. How he had become so attached to Weston so quickly, how it had gone from the instinct to protect the vulnerable to the concern of a friend bemused him. He couldn't trace the path. He only knew that it had settled. His desire for Weston's well-being wasn't centered around his need for Khale to survive or his need for his own survival.

He wanted Weston's lungs to heal for Weston's sake, nothing more. It was the biggest step away from self-centeredness he'd made since his banishment to the Stilts. So much of their life was about survival, about time together before time ran out. That amount of focus on another person was alien to Konrad.

Alien, and absolutely necessary.

"I used to belong to a boys' choir," he admitted to Weston for the sake of distracting him from his pneumonia. "Singing songs about Maelchor while I waited to discover that I was Gancanagh."

"Will you teach me the songs?" Weston asked.

"If you like," he agreed. "There are some others which are more fun." He thought Weston might enjoy some of the more rugged sea shanties.

Konrad had gone to sea with his father twice: once to Angmaan and once to the Dels. In the Isles, everyone still referred to the Dels as Maelmaan, though they'd changed their own name when the twins had split the kingdom in two. It was now called *The Brothers*, and neither brother would relinquish his half to the other.

Angmaan had been a thriving port full of sounds and scents and tastes. His father had taught him which merchants could be trusted. He'd explained about overhead, negotiating, and a good deal of talk about oysters which Konrad hadn't understood.

Maelmaan had been to visit a temple with a group of girls who might become the future keepers of the realm. The temple had been uninteresting, and after Konrad became Gancanagh, he'd always resented the Selkies who ran the temple, for not foreseeing his plight. They'd said he would become a potent influence on the realm, and his father took that to mean he would be a wealthy and powerful merchant.

Now resentment grew into a curiosity which Konrad attempted to dampen. He had no desire to become a *potent influence* on the realm or anything else. He wanted Khale and a simple peace.

"Yeah," Weston said in a way which suggested he'd said it once already and been ignored. Konrad tried to recall what they'd talked of—the songs. He'd promised Weston something fun.

He tried to think of the manliest of all the songs, which was a bit of a mockery of a normal sailor's ways, weighed against the insularity of the Selkie-Gancanagh race.

He sang, softly at first, and then growing louder as he went:

Old Billy McHugh is a lucky fine lad
He can catch any fish from his dory
And give him a line in the pub down the bay
He'll give it right back with a story

Compass(ion)

For Billy's got gold, he's got land, he's got goods
Whatever a lady could dream of
And when Billy sets out in his boat for a tour
The ladies have nothing to scream of

Way-ho, Billy-O
Off in the Dells with the ladies
Way-ho, Billy-O
The Dells are all full of his babies

Old Billy McHugh plays his cards with the men
And plays 'em again with the ladies
The men give him gold and a turn with their wives
And the wives give him nothing but maybes

Way-ho, Billy-O
Off in Nivern with the ladies
Way-ho, Billy-O
Nivern is full of his babies

Old Billy McHugh has a strong stalwart boat
With riggings designed by a master
She'll race any boat under Maelchor's sky
It's a guarantee Billy's is faster

For Billy's got gold, he's got land, he's got goods
Whatever old Billy can dream of
But when Billy goes down in the storm off the point
His fortune is nothing to scream of

Way-ho, Billy-O
Down in the sea with the ladies
Way-ho, Billy-O
The Undine queen won't want his babies

Khale joined in after the first verse, less certain of the melody than Konrad, his sweet voice tentative as he sought the notes.

When Weston joined in the final refrain and then was wrong for the final line, Konrad felt a strange desire to hug him. He'd make a fine singer himself if he chose that route.

And if he and Konrad were to escape, Weston could keep a beat. It could prove useful if they needed to pull the sail and cut quickly across the sea. Feeling the beat in one's bones was critical to coordinated rowing.

Weston's relaxed expression became suddenly tense. He glanced toward the woods to the south and east of them. It was the only warning they received before one of the village men, dressed in a suede vest with a linen tunic and leggings, stepped toward them from the shadows of the trees.

"I thought I heard singing," the man said in a jovial voice.

The knife was in easy reach if Konrad needed it. He suspected the man would be kind long enough to trap them before he attacked or arrested them.

Whatever happened, Konrad wouldn't touch the knife unless Khale or Weston was in danger.

"Welcome," Khale said. He took a step toward the villager. "Would you like some shark?"

"Please," the man said.

They led him through the woods towards the cave. Konrad hung back, in case Weston felt the need to warn or advise him about anything, but Weston walked in silence.

Behind the blind, concealed against the mouth of the cave, all of them took seats around the fire. Khale passed the villager a chunk of shark meat.

"It's been a long walk," the villager said after several bites of food. "What brings you up the mountain?"

Khale rested his hand on Weston's shoulder. "We have been celebrating this young man's birthday. He's 17 now."

The man took several more bites of food. Konrad stood and

traced out a circular path around the fire, which he proceeded to pace while they all waited for the man to decide their fate.

After a moment, shark meat gone, the man asked, "What's it like where you are?"

No one spoke. Konrad couldn't think of a thing to say which wouldn't come off as ungrateful. Khale seemed to be struggling as well.

Weston traced nonsense letters in the dirt with a stick he'd come by somewhere. "It sucks," he complained. "I just got there two days ago." He managed a very theatrical cough for effect.

Konrad grinned and looked away from the fire, out of the villager's vision.

"Some nights," the man confessed, a bit timid, "I wonder if it would be worth it. That's a no, then?"

Khale met Konrad's eyes, their silent vow to each other to never regret the price of their love. Whenever this sort of thing came up, they had only to look at each other to renew that solemn promise.

Khale glanced at the villager. "We all have to choose how we spend our time on this small island of limited opportunity. We've chosen companionship, but we've been outcast from the Stilts for protecting this man who is not like us."

"They're allowed to do that?" the man asked.

No, of course, they weren't permitted to exile anyone. It wasn't as though Ambrose had come along and given Magne or any of the others the right to pass judgment on anyone in the group. They were meant to be exiled together, not scattered around the island.

Konrad laughed at the idea of a group of banished men being allowed to govern themselves. "We'd prefer no one forced them to take us back," he said to the man pointedly.

Khale went on to explain, "Our side of the island does not usually enjoy large meals. The shark is a treat, but with the scarcity of food, they have been unwilling to accept Weston. The village has also rejected him. We're just trying to make do and give him a chance to survive through the winter, so he can leave the island. He isn't one of us."

While Khale spoke, Konrad watched the villager's eyes fall on Weston, taking in the youthful shape of his body and the curve of his hips. Konrad saw the new hunger in the man's eyes and ran his thumb over the hilt of his knife again, thoughtful.

He might not need to use it.

Might.

The villager nodded his head, sympathetic by all appearances. "Florian turned the council against the idea of him." He licked his lips. "I could take him for you. They listen to me."

"No," Weston stated immediately, fierce.

Konrad glanced at Khale to assess his tension. It was there in his eyes and in the stretch of his lips, but the rest of his body and face appeared relaxed. The villager probably had no idea how alert and protective Khale had just become.

The villager shrugged his shoulders, also apparently relaxed. He played a dark game, circling for the kill.

For a moment, Konrad toyed with the idea: what was one sexual encounter that weighed in the balance against Khale's life?

He met Khale's eyes again, and Khale gave a subtle shake of his head.

Khale knew. Either he'd guessed, or overheard them talking, or Weston had told him while Konrad slept. Whatever had passed, Khale knew that Weston expected him to die, and he was saying *no* to Konrad's debate about the value of a life.

Weston mattered more to Khale than his own life.

Konrad shouldn't have been surprised, but the realization stung, nonetheless. "Guess you don't want to go home then," he said.

"I want to go home," Weston asserted. "But I will stay with them to get there."

The villager inched toward Weston. He seemed to believe, perhaps, that some sort of physical contact might sway Weston's opinion of how safe he was.

"I understand," the villager said. "I used to be scared of older men too." He put his hand on Weston's forearm possessively. Konrad thumbed the knife and listened as the villager continued. "It's safe. I won't hurt you. My name is Tomlin. I used to be your age; I remember."

"You might not want to hurt me," Weston said. He either played dumb, or he was too naive to realize what the man, Tomlin, wanted from him. "But these people won't listen to you. I just need a boat. I can leave, and no one has to get in each other's way."

Tomlin stood. It was a good position, Konrad thought. He would perceive Konrad as the primary threat, if he tried to attack Weston, and would underestimate Khale because he was sitting. Khale could charge him from below; he would have a firmer foundation from which to hold a position against Tomlin until Konrad could mitigate him.

"I can get you a boat," Tomlin told Weston. He offered his hand to pull the boy up, but Weston folded his arms across his chest.

"Can you leave it down there?" he asked. He nodded in the direction of the shoreline.

"Sure," Tomlin promised. He leaned down toward Weston. Konrad pulled the knife from his pocket, ready.

All Tomlin did was tickle Weston's side a bit. It was an unusual, confusing move. Konrad would have liked to know what Khale thought of it, but he didn't want to take his eyes off Tomlin to read Khale's expression.

"See?" Tomlin teased. "Nothing to be afraid of." He tickled Weston's side again.

Weston drew his body away from Tomlin's easy reach, toward the fire. Konrad suspected he might be preparing himself to pull a stick from the fire if it seemed that Tomlin would refuse to leave him alone. Perhaps he understood what Tomlin wanted after all.

"When you get back to the village," Weston said with force, "and you decide who to tell about me, remember I have a chance to live. And they've," he pointed to Khale and Konrad, "done nothing except keep me safe. If you are wise, you could be free of this island someday. I won't forget you."

"I won't tell anyone in the village about you, Weston," Tomlin assured him. He stepped toward him again, into the heat of the fire.

"Or them," Weston insisted.

Tomlin nodded his head eagerly. "Or them. I want your friends safe. I can see that you care about them." He put his hand on Weston's shoulder. "Safe, all of you," he said tenderly. He offered his other hand to Weston. "Will you help me move the boat?"

Weston brushed Tomlin's hand off his shoulder. "And I like women," he stated.

"How do you know?" Tomlin argued.

"I am betrothed to a princess," Weston announced. It was news to Konrad — disturbing news, though Konrad could not place why. "I like her," he added.

Tomlin was silent for a moment, studying Weston.

He stepped away from the fire decisively. "I understand," he said. "I'll get that boat for you." He turned and walked around the blind, towards the woods and the flatland below.

Konrad wondered whether this was a network of caves. If so, they could retreat into the darkness with their fire and hide, or emerge elsewhere in the hills. They ought to have explored deeper into the cave, but Konrad misliked the labored state of Weston's breathing. He returned the knife to his pocket safely.

"What is he going to do?" Khale asked.

Rather than answer him, Weston waited, his head cocked to one side.

A moment later, Konrad realized why: Tomlin's voice yelled, "Men! There are men hiding in the caves! Criminals!"

Weston sighed, which turned into a fit of coughing. "That," he said, once he could breathe again.

Konrad looked at them both and then let his eyes rest on Khale's face. "I'll go towards them," he offered. "You should conceal yourselves."

Weston shook his head. "It won't matter. Your only chance is if you head into the ocean."

The ocean. A jump from the cliffs could prove fatal, never mind the tumultuous waters below. "How will we be safe that way?"

Konrad countered incredulously. It wasn't possible that Weston's Luck would tell him it was the best alternative.

"I don't know," Weston snapped, "but it's his only way." He pointed toward Khale with his thumb before marching out of the cave on a determined course.

"Let's go, then," Konrad said to Khale. He grabbed the medical kit, which Weston would certainly need after another swim, and followed Weston out of the cave.

Out of the cave and into a group of a half dozen men, who had surrounded Weston. They surrounded Konrad and Khale as well, and a pair of them held Konrad's arms behind his back in a painful grasp. Khale seemed to be in a similar situation.

Weston, they let stand free. He gazed at the group a moment before he addressed the one he must have concluded was the leader. "Deyton, Negash. What kind of name is that? Let us go."

"Why are you out of your area?" the one he'd called Deyton asked. He wore the same attire as Tomlin, although he was more naturally fit.

"They tried to rape me!" Tomlin accused.

Konrad rolled his eyes at the absurdity of it all. If Khale died, it was going to be because people were inherently stupid and inherently selfish.

"No, they didn't," Weston argued. "He's hiding his own interest in men, and I refused to go with him."

"At four hundred," Deyton countered, a small smile on his face, "Tomlin suddenly developed an interest?" He nodded his head at the men holding Konrad and again at the two who held Khale.

Someone clasped linked metal cuffs around Konrad's wrists, binding his arms and hands behind his back.

He looked at Khale. "Don't fight them," he asked. "Please."

Khale assured him that he wouldn't.

"No," Weston informed Deyton, snide. "He suddenly had a boy in the woods to prey on."

So much for Konrad's theory that Weston was naive.

"The man is vulgar," Tomlin complained. "You should send him back to the Stilts."

Deyton looked around at the gathered guards. Then, he looked at Weston. Then Khale. Then Konrad. He paused, either for thought or theatrics, before he announced, "The decision is ultimately up to Ambrose." He looked at Weston, sincere. "Do we need to tie you too, or will you obey?"

"I'll obey," Weston said.

Well done.

Deyton nodded towards Tomlin. "Arrest him too. Ambrose will want to hear both sides."

One of the men slipped linked metal cuffs around Tomlin's wrists. Tomlin made a show of not resisting.

Deyton gave the orders for them to move across the mountain and toward the village on the far side.

Konrad hadn't been there in nearly a thousand years. He let his mind wander back to what memories he had of the place: the well-constructed wood-frame buildings, the streets paved in small stones, the cottages which housed six men each in solitary bedrooms with small common areas, the dining hall, the school, the room where scrolls were reproduced.

When he pictured that last room, he could still smell the unique blend of pressed paper and fresh ink, could still hear the scratching of quills against the page.

He half-listened, and half-remembered as they descended the hills, listening while Deyton and Weston got to know each other. Weston managed to get Deyton to laugh a few times, but the more Deyton seemed to like Weston, the more outraged Tomlin seemed. When Weston mentioned the gold they'd found in the mountain the other day, Tomlin's nostrils flared with rage.

While Deyton grilled Weston on the nature of Konrad's and Khale's respective characters, Konrad leaned his head toward Khale.

"We'll find a way out of this," he promised with false confidence.

"No matter what," Khale said in an urgent tone, "protecting him was worth it."

"It could cost us our lives," Konrad argued, frustrated.

Perhaps Weston's life was worth the price of Khale's. Perhaps Khale's life was the more valuable one. It didn't matter in the great scheme; they shouldn't ever have needed to make that choice.

Konrad vowed if he did somehow escape to ensure that no one had to make that sort of decision again.

"It may," Khale agreed, "but our lives aren't worth much here."

Konrad closed his eyes. Khale's life was worth everything to him. He wished there was a way for Khale to see that and understand.

"His is worth something, somewhere better than this," Khale added.

Konrad glanced at him. "I'd hug you if I could," he teased.

It wasn't fully teasing, save the tone. He longed for every hug with Khale that he was never going to get. Millions of lost moments, stacking up together, attempting to compress themselves into this one span of time, so brief, buried in the chaos of a few intense days.

"My memories will never forget the comfort of your embrace," Khale whispered.

Konrad laughed, low and deep. "I do love you," he told Khale. Let the guards who led them be disgusted by their conversation. It didn't matter. "Always."

"I love you too," Khale breathed. "Always."

Maorekel—always—was a long time. Forever apart—if Weston's prediction came true. Konrad at least would have a life—or a semblance of one—but Khale would be on his own, wherever it was that the dead went to rest their souls.

He breathed a prayer to Maelchor. He'd never had the best relationship with the god, but now he begged and pleaded and promised to do anything in exchange for Khale's life.

Maelchor had a funny way of remaining silent, which irked Konrad.

He recalled Weston's promise to answer any questions he asked in the future, and he mulled over the differences between men and gods and the value of faith and trust. Silence and action.

He knew where his faith lay, in the end.

19

WESTON

If Weston were to lie to himself, he would say he had been resting quietly to give Konrad and Khale the space they needed to talk. He wouldn't admit his brief break from living had anything to do with the pain searing through his flesh, the ache throbbing in his chest, an inability to breathe except for small bubbles of air within the crevices of fluid that had built back up, or the fever that was raging through his body like the infernos of a fire fairy set to take vengeance.

Since they'd arrived in the village, they'd been inside a single small room. There wasn't space for privacy, let alone to relieve oneself without another being able to see you. It was a new level of dismal.

"Are you alright, Weston?" Khale asked.

"Yes. I feel great," Weston replied. His voice was more strained than he intended, and Khale's eyes studied him more closely.

Great amounts of agony, great amounts of pain, great amounts of frustration, great amounts of disappointment.

Weston felt *great*, but not in the way his response implied.

"He's been struggling since before we left the Stilts," Khale reminded Konrad.

Konrad locked his square jaw and tight eyes on Weston. "I'd like to check on things."

Konrad set his icy hands on Weston's back and began knocking against his chest as Ambrose had done.

"He's alert. That's something," Khale remarked.

"I'm very alert," Weston said for himself, so they wouldn't forget he was there, alive, part of the conversation.

On the matter of being alive, Weston realized he had made a fatal flaw in his last few uses of his skill set. He had used Luck to be charming, but it hadn't saved them. They were still progressing toward something that felt catastrophic. He had decided, when the men surrounded them, to follow an alternative route: He would ask Luck what to do to get him off the island safely. Luck wanted that. It was his supposed destiny, so following it might go better than trying to navigate the momentary crises that he faced around every corner of life on the island.

Konrad's hand pressed against Weston's shoulder. Weston looked up at him.

"Weston."

Weston puffed his lips out. "Konrad," he mimicked, though his tone was surlier.

Konrad's hand remained on Weston, but it slid more toward his back. The touch was lighter and comforting.

"Which is greater?" Konrad asked. "Your fear of pain or the pain itself?"

"The compilation is a fear worth lying over," Weston replied.

His breathing had become so shallow he was supplementing the quick breaths with more painful, deep ones. He felt faint and wanted to sleep. He was tired of fighting for his life on this island that didn't want him, his intuition, or any other part of himself.

"Plus, I think I might like death," he added. If he died, he could visit with people he wanted to see. It was a brilliant plan, except most of the people he wanted to see were still alive.

"If that's so, then why have you spent so long avoiding it? Lie down."

Fear, in some regards, was a driving factor in Weston's inability to want to move forward in life. Fear, he knew, would keep paralyzing him unless he took control of it, though to think of doing something is quite different than doing it.

"I'm fine," Weston replied. "I feel great."

He was back to what type of great he felt, and Khale was laughing from his corner of the room.

Konrad set a hand against his upper back and another on his chest and moved Weston to a lying position; he didn't protest yet, but he had a plan to roll away if it became necessary.

Except rolling would further ruin his stitches.

He knew he would allow Konrad to do this. He knew it was necessary. He knew, but he hated it.

"Then there's no harm in letting me listen to your chest," Konrad said, like he didn't know what the outcome would be.

"You're a worthy adversary," Weston replied. He aided Konrad in lying the rest of the way down, and this time, he earned a genuine laugh from Khale.

Konrad did what all people buying time do: He listened to his chest far longer than necessary.

Then, he sat back and looked at Weston. "I haven't got a stick this time."

The men of the village had let them keep their belongings — assuming they were unarmed, Weston guessed — but they hadn't brought a stick with them.

"Looks like we're waiting it out then?" Weston hoped.

Khale moved across the room to the other side of Weston.

"Would you prefer Khale or I hold you?" Konrad asked.

Weston preferred to die.

No, Weston preferred to be without pain. He didn't want to die or go through the agony of an operation—with or without the stick. He didn't care about the stick.

The stick was important. He needed a channel for his pain. He looked through the room for something he could hold on to, squeeze, anything.

Real jails had bars. Their cell was simply a room barricaded on the outside.

Weston looked between the two men, with no solution for how to cope with the pain during the operation except to be restrained from doing anything at all. His best hope was to have it done quickly, with hands that didn't shake or lack confidence.

He looked at Konrad. "I think the better question is: Would I prefer Khale or you stick a pipe inside my chest? I don't know if I'm feeling that lucky these days..."

Khale placed his hand on Weston, without warning or any chance for Weston to escape. "I'll hold him down. You saw the procedure before."

"We could leave it and see what happens," Konrad replied, his hands sifting through the bag of materials they were so generously, and luckily, left. "I'm not sure I feel that lucky either."

Weston did not appreciate Konrad's humor. "Great," he replied.

Khale pinned Weston, so he couldn't move. There would be no chance for Weston to even flinch or scurry away.

Khale hummed another tune in his ear while Konrad focused on the procedure.

Weston wept in agony as the pipe drove into his body and forced fluid out. He breathed in air that filled his lung as it pressed itself against the pipe, wedged just underneath it.

He felt everything, each second of agonizing pain, but he latched onto the sound too.

Seaward and skyward and down to the earth,
Flows like a river across your hearth.
Onto the ocean and cross the wide sea
Led by the moonlight
To prosper in dreams
We look to the heavens
And ask for your gold
To grant us a bounty
As we live by your words

Deep in the earth
We uncover our dreams
And look to the stars
As we cross rivers and streams
Mountains will see us up into your arms
But deep underneath we may burn with your scorn
Infernos will see us into a new life
By may we never forget your dear lady wife.
Seaward and skyward and down to the earth
Flows like a river across your hearth
Onto the ocean and cross the wide sea
Led by the moonlight
To prosper in dreams
Seaward and skyward and down to the earth
We burn with our passion
And drown by our curse

The sound of Khale's voice rumbling inside his chest drifted with the pain. Weston leaned back, blinking.

"Alright?" Konrad asked.

Weston closed his eyes and leaned against Khale's chest, too tired to reply.

Khale's hand brushed over Weston's scalp. "Let him rest."

"There's a medicine he needs," Konrad insisted. "They must have it here somewhere. I remember when my grandfather was ill, they'd made something from mold and given it to him. The mold killed whatever curse set the water in his lungs."

The room was silent, almost as though they had left. Weston drifted across the water and back to the arms of his mother, which were less encompassing than Konrad's.

"We can't continue living like this," Khale's voice said, growing from the silence into something resolved and firm. It was something unique to Khale from what Weston knew of him. "But they will take him in."

Weston choked up a painful laugh. "Says the guy with Luck."

"We'll have to tell Ambrose which medicine he needs," Konrad said, his hand soothing as it ran down Weston's arm.

Once his recent cough subsided, and the pain ebbed into an ache, he let his eyes drift in the warmth of the two men taking care of him, providing more support in his struggle than his parents had given him.

"I would like some more soup, please," Weston joked.

"I'll ask the next person who comes in," Konrad replied.

Weston felt things shifting, the certainty of anything lost to him, and his intuition no longer the only pull towards the two men.

Luck, the more he understood it, was not Luck at all. It was a predisposition to being fortunate, to seeing potential. It was a silent companion. Others had discredited these two, but Weston felt their potential, and he could see ways to shape them toward something useful, instead of the same monotonous struggle they had been stuck in, tumbling like weeds in the island's vacuum.

He closed his eyes, sensing they had time before anyone would come to see him, and shifted, so once again they could have their time together, without the obvious intrusion Weston had created in their lives.

20

KONRAD

Weston slept. Konrad leaned against the wall, Khale's body flush against his, their faces nearly side-by-side.

"You did a good job," Khale murmured.

They both peered across the room, watching the even rise and fall of Weston's chest.

Konrad laid back. He decided they needed to leave here with four things in order of priority: Khale, the mold-based medicine, the necklace, and the knife. Weston seemed to believe they needed a boat, which amused Konrad. On some level, that was the same as saying they'd need air to breathe.

There was a distinction—they'd need to obtain the boat. Air came free by virtue of existing everywhere, but the boat would have to be found and moved. With a sigh, he added it to his mental list, between Weston's medicine and the necklace. Everything else could be left behind if necessary.

"As did you," Konrad whispered against Khale's neck. "He trusts you."

Khale leaned against him, feeling more relaxed. "Do you ever wish our fate did not restrict us from parenthood?"

Konrad played with the tendrils of his hair where they clung to the back of his neck. It had been centuries, but Khale was still tormented by his past.

Konrad's Gancanagh curse had become apparent at the birthday celebration of his betrothed. She'd screamed, calling the attention of all in attendance. He'd never had a moment to consider hiding it, nor was he given time to adjust to the reality before he faced the accusations and loathing of the adults he trusted. The girl had died. Konrad had been banished. End of story.

It had not been so for Khale. He'd made an effort to hide the curse. Though it was forbidden, he'd sneaked away with the girl. They'd attempted to make a life together—so young and so alone. Their families had searched for them, found them, and separated them. She and their daughter had been executed to prevent their genetics from spreading. Khale had been banished.

Perhaps Khale hungered for redemption?

All of them did in their way. Khale had his girl Fennery, and their daughter, Ketty. Konrad had his girl, Leila.

All of them on this island were killers, save Weston.

He ran his hands down Khale's arms, comforting him. "I think you're a strong example to him. Don't ever think you aren't a parent, even if he is full grown. Wherever he goes, whatever he does with his freedom, you'll always be his father in a way."

Khale angled his face toward Konrad. "I know you expect me to die soon—that he has seen it."

So Konrad was right; Khale knew. He'd already insisted that Weston's life meant more to him than his own with no regard for what Konrad's feelings on the matter might be.

"Did you guess it or overhear us?" Konrad asked him. He kept his hands on Khale's body. The need to be touching him had grown exponentially since the start of this conversation.

"I guessed," Khale said. "You've been acting odd. Protective to an extreme."

How could he not?

He cupped Khale's face in his left hand and urged him to turn so that they faced one another. When Khale was settled again, cross-legged in the nest of Konrad's open legs, Konrad spoke. "They've taken your time, your choices, your health. I won't let anyone take the rest of your future, whatever it may be."

"And if it comes to it," Khale offered. Tears flooded his eyes as he regarded Konrad and struggled to put to words whatever sentiment he felt. "This isn't much of a life," he managed at last. His voice broke on the final word.

Konrad drew him into a tight hug, ran his hands through his hair and down his back. "It's ours," he told Khale with conviction. "It's what we have." He kissed him.

To his surprise, given the situation, Khale returned the kiss with passion, his hands on Konrad's thigh and in his hair, his body moving closer until he was all but on top of Konrad, kissing. Konrad ran his hands down Khale's back, pulling their bodies together.

The deep well of yearning which had grown within him over the past few days now threatened to overwhelm his common sense, which told him they were in enough danger as it was.

He and Khale pulled away from each other in mutual dissatisfaction.

Breathing heavily, Konrad struggled to focus his thoughts on something coherent, something worthwhile.

He settled on a story.

"My father told me a story about a fish when I was a boy. Once, there was a fish who would swim up to the ports to see what the sailors unloaded from their ships. He watched ship after ship being unloaded and wondered why he had no possessions, so he went to Maelchor and demanded to know why he was given an existence with so few options, with no ownership, with nothing that is *his*. Maelchor told him that the sea was his. He had given him the entire ocean. The fish argued and asked for possessions. So, Maelchor gave him the gold and the statues that he had asked for and put him back in the sea. The fish couldn't swim with everything weighing him down. He had everything he wanted, but he couldn't swim."

He met Khale's eyes. "You are my ocean," he told him ardently.

Khale kissed him again, in answer.

"Do you miss being a merchant's son?" Khale asked him.

"No," Konrad answered with a laugh. "I would have made a terrible merchant." He grinned knowingly at Khale. "People mislike me," he teased.

Khale laughed in agreement, massaging Konrad's back.

"Do you miss your life?" Konrad asked him. He tried to imagine Khale as an artisan with a talent for some product or another rather than as someone struggling to survive.

"I miss parts of it," Khale admitted. "I don't think I would have appreciated it, though. It would have felt like a punishment."

They both softly laughed at that. Yes, being a merchant, marrying a girl—it would have felt like a punishment to Konrad. He understood.

"I have a good life here," Khale finished, "despite everything. A peaceful life. Most of it, at least."

Konrad laughed. Until this week, their lives had been more dull and pointless than peaceful. They'd been surviving, not living. Now they had purpose, direction, intent beyond mere subsistence.

"This week has been a mess." He tucked some of Khale's hair back from his face and murmured, "Whatever happens, whether his prediction is correct or not, I'll be there for him in whatever way I can."

"You would make a good father, if you could see him that way." Khale kissed Konrad and then pulled away, sitting beside him now. "What is our plan?"

From across the room came Weston's voice, fuzzy and vague in tone but direct in wording. "Your uncle was killed. His necklace is with Ambrose, and we're going to take it and leave."

His uncle. Shock coursed through Konrad. Violence over the necklace was unsurprising. His uncle likely didn't deserve it.

"All of us?" Konrad asked pointedly.

"I don't think so," Weston said. "But I won't give up."

If he couldn't find a solution, why did he have to be awake? Why interrupt their solace for nothing?

He pressed the heels of his hands into his eyes, struggling to focus his mind on something besides the rage that coursed through him. None of this was Weston's fault. He had the right to wake or sleep as he pleased.

Konrad wasn't ready to be done talking to Khale alone. That wasn't Weston's fault. It was the world's.

A moment later, he calmed. He couldn't let his fear of losing Khale turn him into someone he wasn't, into a man who would take his fear out on an innocent and frightened young man. Weston had stepped up and become someone new for Khale's sake, and Konrad ought not belittle that growth over a moment's frustration.

He breathed deeply and turned toward Weston. "Where does Ambrose have the necklace?"

"In the stores," Weston said after a moment of quiet thought.

"Given the situation," Konrad mused, "I think he'll share it. Khale and I can take turns with it and live somewhere secluded." He smiled toward Khale. "But we can have lives. Adopt sons if we like."

Khale returned the smile, half-hopeful. "How are we going to do this?" he asked. "Request it?"

"I think Ambrose might have less of a headache if we were off the island," Konrad explained. Three of them, banished from both communities...what would Ambrose do with them? He'd either have to break long-established rules, kill them all, or set them free. Ambrose was not a killer.

"I agree," Khale said. He stood. "We can ask him."

Weston grinned at them both, a healthier grin than he'd worn in more than a day. "The good news is, he might say yes."

21

WESTON

They were taken by a guard who didn't have any manners. He offered not his name nor his conversation while they were escorted to a large domed room. Based on what he could see of the village during their descent from the ridge, Weston guessed that all of the important spaces were dome-shaped. Luck agreed.

This room had a series of chairs in rows. At the front, one chair stood above the rest. Ambrose there, his back straighter than his hobbling implied was possible. It was a stark contrast to the usual rounded, time-worn shape Ambrose had presented on the hillside. Weston wonder how old he was, and if some of his movements were an act.

Luck said he was no more than four-thousand-years. Not quite at the halfway point of his expected lifespan.

Here, Ambrose was the leader. Each wrinkle sagged around his eyes like a ring on a tree. He was their keeper of the wisest thoughts and a voice among hundreds of philosophers.

Alongside him, Deyton sat with various other men.

Konrad, Khale, and Weston sat at the front of the room, at a table adorned with water and light refreshments.

Weston waited while the room filled with standing men. They each had seats, but none chose to sit. None of them took the food either.

Finally, Ambrose knocked his mallet on the table. The various conversations faded into a respectful silence.

"Everyone is here," Ambrose announced. "We can begin."

Weston took a moment, while the room settled, to look around and see who *everyone* was. At a table near them, Goran and Magne sat. Tomlin was opposite them, on the far side of the front row. The men from the village were all well-dressed and healthy, while those from the Stilts were bony and waxen by comparison, their clothes barely more than rags.

"Good evening," Weston said.

Ambrose's lip twitched, and his eyebrows raised as he took in Weston. Weston imagined he looked rather worn by this point in his adventures on the island. It was a good thing, he suspected, because he needed to look pitiful in the eyes of his jury.

"How is your illness, young man?" Ambrose asked.

"My illness is flourishing," Weston replied.

"He needs a mold-based medicine to destroy the fluid," Konrad insisted.

"It's expensive and hard to come by," Ambrose lied. "We'll exhaust other options first."

Weston was exhausted. Two pipes in the chest and he was about ready to maul someone for suggesting there was an easier—or harder—option they should try before resorting to the medicine Ambrose had and could make more of. It was mold. A skilled hand could make non-lethal mold anytime, with the right tools and setting.

Perhaps Weston was being too dramatic. After all, the study of medicine was a refined and fragile field of the sciences. Wyvern didn't study science at all and if he had been home he would have died.

A feeling washed over Weston: The island had saved him from a fate more painful than his brother taking his life. A fate he wouldn't have faced if he had never been shipwrecked. Was it the cost of his life? This suffering, this struggle. Surely nothing came free in life.

He had paid in blood.

Weston glanced at Deyton, a man he thought had a strong sense of values and had enjoyed his company. Weston liked him and felt a potential to get off the island through his aid.

"It's more expensive than my passage off the island?" Weston surmised. "If you could send me with escorts, I can navigate the wards the Selkies have in place, and you wouldn't have to exhaust anything."

"They have no means of leaving the island, unfortunately," Ambrose retorted.

You have a boat, Weston thought. He glanced at Konrad and Khale, who shared a look. He bet they were thinking the same thing.

Ambrose continued, "Some crimes have been levied against them, which they must answer for."

Konrad lurched to his feet. "Khale did nothing. Any transgressions were my actions alone."

Despite his wish to take all responsibility, to give his life to protect Khale, Luck said it would never work. "They want Khale dead, so Magne can lead unopposed. You have the necklace." Weston stated.

"The necklace?" Ambrose asked. "I burned it, as I said I would. It has caused too much strife already. We are a peaceful society."

Weston knew the second he said the necklace had been burned that its existence continued just as the boat's did.

He also realized it was better to not say anything than to amplify the unsettled energy of the room. People would demand to know what the necklace meant. It would detract from things. At this juncture, to know it was not burned was enough. To find it could come later. Plus, he already had a suspicion of where it was held.

Ambrose turned his attention toward Florian, the man who had denied him access to the village days ago. "You say these men, Konrad and Khale, injured the young man, Weston?"

"I think most, if not all, of the men in the Stilts did."

Was it a lie, if Florian believed it?

"And I think sharks can walk," Weston proclaimed. "Any other absurd claims?"

"I never touched him," Magne said from his corner of the room.

"I find it alarming that two separate parties have accused you of moral misconduct. One could be a matter of misunderstanding, but two?" Ambrose asked Konrad and Khale. His eyes lingered on Khale's face, searching.

Konrad's fate went from imminent death to possible life in a fraction of a second. Why, Weston did not know.

Khale's life still felt hopeless; Weston tried not to dwell on something he did not see the point in trying to change anymore.

"You don't find it alarming that it's an easy conclusion for any of them to draw?" Konrad asked, his voice going from the brashness that would have had him killed to a softer, more pleading question.

"I have never forced myself on another," Khale stated. "Nor have I been with any male other than Konrad. I am guilty of finding a helpless young man, barely out of boyhood, and wanting to help him. I am being accused of crimes for the first time in over a thousand years for the first time beyond my status as a Gancanagh. No one misliked me until I protected him. My history is sound. I've never stirred anything up nor violated anyone's rights. I see him as a son, not anything more."

"I am accused of killing Urial," Konrad said. "And I don't deny it. Neither of them had any hand in it."

Ambrose looked toward Magne and Goran. "Do you dispute his claim?"

Weston prayed to Maelchor that Goran would be reasonable for once and would not fabricate an exaggeration that would get Khale in more trouble than he was just by sitting in the chair of the accused.

"Khale," Goran said, each sound of the name flowed from his lips with articulation Weston knew was fabricated for the emotional impact of it. "Caused the escalation. He would not have killed Urial otherwise. It would have been a minor fight."

Khale shifted, and Konrad's chair skidded on the floor just enough for Weston to notice but not enough for many others to. They were prepared to move quickly, if needed. The room breathed a sigh as Weston felt the penetrating eyes of everyone fixate on their small table, more than any other moment.

They wanted Khale to be guilty; they wanted someone to be guilty.

Weston couldn't figure out why.

"What about him?" Ambrose asked with a nod toward Weston. He was still calm, still himself, navigating the situation with the ease of a dagger set to destroy Konrad's faith in others.

"We will care for him through winter," Goran promised.

Use, he meant. Not sexually like the villagers feared, but for Luck. For the food he could bring them and the gold he could find them.

"No!" Tomlin, the man who had wanted to use Weston for his own satisfaction, exclaimed. "He threw himself at me and tried to seduce me! He should be punished, not set free!"

The absurdity of the claim astonished Weston; the Stilts were anything but free.

"You don't think the Stilts are punishment enough?" Ambrose asked.

"I...." Tomlin said, his face turning a shade of red. He wanted Weston for himself, not for the Stilts. "It is."

Tomlin sat back in his chair, resigned.

"Weston," Ambrose stated, standing and reclaiming his rounded shape. "You are hereby exiled to the Stilts. You may not travel the island, nor use any hunting tools, nor attempt to leave the island. Doing so will result in death. Do you understand?"

The most insane of men would have trouble understanding why they were not allowed to fend for themselves, especially when they were starving.

"Why can't I hunt?" Weston asked.

"Shortened rations are part of the punishment. If you hunt your own food, what lesson do you learn?"

He had a few lessons to derive from the experience, like fending for himself because no one would help him survive, or the value of companionship because he would be alone for the winter if he stayed.

"Then kill me. I don't accept it."

He didn't plan to remain on the island long enough for this to even be an argument. He couldn't resist the argument, despite himself: the absurdity of the treatment toward the men of the Stilts, the idea of sentencing a dying person to die *there* instead of here...It was all pointless suffering.

Can't use hunting tools? What high horse were they perched on that they would deny another the opportunity to feed himself?

There were types of murder, and denying food was one.

"You may kill yourself if you desire," Ambrose said. "But that is not an appropriate punishment for your behavior."

Banishment was death, given his illness.

"Well, I don't accept it, and I will hunt."

Ambrose sighed. "It is your choice." He resettled himself in his judgment chair, straightened his shoulders, and watched his hands as he spread them across the expanse of his table for a moment. He looked up again, toward Konrad and Khale. "Did you kill Urial?"

Konrad met him with the same firmness. "Khale slept during the attack. The blame lies with me."

"No. I didn't," Khale said.

Konrad put his hand on Khale's. "Don't."

"I think you should take a moment," Khale demanded. "To realize that death, even one of us, does not change that others will die soon. Does not change that we refuse to live any longer under your *shortened rations* and that you will never control us with your punishments."

Weston suspected Konrad wanted to tell Khale to shut up twice as much as Weston did himself.

"Your opinion is noted," Ambrose replied.

The room was silent; Ambrose read a paper set in front of him. "It says here that Urial's throat was slit with a knife? Where did you get a knife?"

"I found it," Konrad replied, his pitch raised and light, hollow.

The betrayal stung them both: Konrad from familiarity and

Weston from compassion, a place where he watched Konrad lose the pillars of his strength.

"Beside my body," Weston added. "It was mine until you decided to control us. I warned you when you taught him how to do the first surgery: you've dug your own grave, Ambrose."

Ambrose frowned—Weston suspected from the revelation of his own activities, but Weston didn't care. Konrad didn't seem to either.

"The council will take a day to decide your punishment," Ambrose declared. "Does anyone have anything to add?"

Weston glanced toward Deyton. Luck hinted at things Deyton wanted from life, beliefs Deyton held about this trial. "You won't build the future you want here if you punish any of us."

Deyton's shoulders fell in submission. "It isn't up to me."

"Take Weston to the Stilts please," Ambrose said to Deyton. "And return them to their room," he commanded Florian.

Weston stayed in his seat as the room cleared and hushed voices rose, each commenting on the trial, what had come of it, and what they expected to come of the next day's verdict.

Tomlin sat, a smile spread across his face. Despite being accused of crimes, he was set free.

No, Weston sensed they would address him more discreetly. The village did not demand—nor want to see—one of their own sentenced to a crime. They trusted each other; Weston could sense the network between them.

Weston understood why Konrad caused such difficulty for the village: he had lied about himself and gained the trust of many of the men in the room. Now he had lost that trust; he had lost them.

Konrad and Khale left the room once most everyone else had gone, and finally, Deyton stood.

22

KONRAD

There was no time for reaction or regret. Florian, of all people, approached them and returned them in ceremonious silence to the room where they'd been.

The blood from Weston's latest surgery still stained the floor.

Konrad was certain these were the final moments of Khale's life. Whatever Ambrose and the council decided, it would not play out in their favor. Konrad peered at him in the half-light of the room. His skin was pale and coated in the labor of the past few days.

If life were not cruel, they could bathe together, relax, and enjoy the luxury of this place in peace.

Khale bridged the space between them and kissed him. Konrad felt the tension in his every muscle, the determination of his hands and his mind. Khale pulled away and leaned his forehead against Konrad's.

"What do we do," he joked, "without our compass?"

Konrad laughed. Khale...he couldn't bear to lose him. He wouldn't survive this.

"We're not staying here," Konrad decided. He pulled away from Khale and looked to the window for some sort of breach on the locking mechanism or a weakness in the structure. He could break the window if he had to, but it would draw attention to their escape.

He felt Khale's hand clasp his and pull him away from the window, towards the pair of chairs and the table in the center of the room. "You're afraid," he accused Konrad.

"You aren't?" he countered.

Every part of him thrummed with the tension of these moments, the building pressure to save Khale, to not make the decision that would cost his life, to get them both out of here.

"I'm often afraid," Khale mused. He met Konrad's eyes. "But you aren't usually so frantic."

That was because Khale's life had always been in a perilous place, but his death had never been a certainty until now. And, though it was selfish, Konrad had always assumed that anything that killed Khale would kill him. It alarmed him to confess to himself that he was more comfortable with Khale's death if it resulted in his own death as well.

It returned him to the cyclical musings of what sort of man he was.

"Am I frantic?" he raised his hand to Khale's upper arm and lowered it again as tears filled his eyes. "I cannot lose you, Khale," he admitted.

Khale embraced him with a small laugh which became a sob. "I don't want to die either," he said, when both breathed evenly again. "But I'm more likely to die when you react to fear than if you plan something." He held Konrad at arm's length and asked, voice steady, "What is worse: the pain or the fear of the pain?"

Konrad laughed, recalling his words to Weston before his second surgery.

"This isn't how we've survived our lives," Khale pressed. "Running at each opportunity because it's convenient. You're smarter than this."

Konrad took in a deep breath while he organized his thoughts into a tidy row of desperation and pinpointed the source of his terror: he had no means of knowing which decision would lead to Khale's death.

"What would you have me do?" he asked Khale. Perhaps, if it were Khale's choice and not Konrad's, the burden would be lessened enough to let him think.

"Take a moment to think," Khale urged, "before jumping out a window."

Konrad forced himself to sit and was relieved when Khale joined him. They could take their way through a plan—weigh and discuss their options, until they found something both were comfortable with.

"Alright," he said. "They have Weston. We're trapped, with a probable unhappy outcome."

Khale reached for his hands. "If it's probable, avoiding it will cause problems. Without considering my potential fate, what would you do?"

Whatever it took. Anything...

"I would give Weston better odds of a successful rescue than us having a successful escape." Really, the most logical thing to do would be to wait there and hope that Weston found them before anyone else came for them.

It bothered Konrad to devise a plan of inaction.

"But he believes you are successful," Khale argued. He glanced out the window. "We should head toward the bay. But we need to get your uncle's talisman."

No, if they left this room, villagers would recognize them. They stood out too much to be able to casually walk around. "Whatever we do," he argued, "Weston will know we're doing it. And we're safer where they want us for now than elsewhere. So, unless someone comes to separate us, what do you say we stay?"

To Konrad's surprise, Khale shook his head. They rarely contradicted one another. Old habit and familiarity left them working in tandem, often going hours without speaking to one another.

He looked at Khale, waiting for more.

"I don't think we should stay," Khale began. "Weston will struggle to get to us here, but he can predict where we will be. We should make it easier for him to find us."

He wanted to leave this room. Its sole virtue seemed to be that no one here wanted to kill either of them, and venture into the uncertainty of the village, where they might be recognized at any moment. Where they *would* be recognized.

It was his life, his decision. It had to be. Konrad was determined to support whatever actions Khale thought were best. "Alright," he agreed. "The bay, then?" He assessed Khale for a moment—haggard and drawn from decades of malnourishment. His appearance stood out too much.

"I have the knife," Konrad mused. "We ought to trim our hair, so we don't stand out as much."

Khale sat and looked up at him with those steady, trusting eyes he had. Khale didn't trust many people, but he trusted Konrad with all of his self. Konrad was paralyzed with a strange fear of letting Khale down, of being the one to fail him and ultimately cause his death.

"I love you," Khale assured him. "No matter what happens, I will always love you."

Konrad nearly laughed. He focused on the task at hand instead, cutting away a large swath of Khale's hair with a sweeping motion. "I believe we established that," he teased. He made another slice at Khale's hair. "Wouldn't it be sad if the knife slipped now?" he thought aloud. What a terrible irony that would be.

Khale laughed. "It would."

Konrad stepped back and admired the youthful change in Khale's features. The shorter hair and beard took at least a century off his appearance. It was a shame his clothing was so spoilt. That alone would make him stand out.

Konrad peered around the room and fixed his eyes on the linen curtains, which hung limp on either side of the window. No doubt they insulated and blocked away the setting sun, but for now...

He tore one side down and trimmed it with his knife so that there was a hole for Khale's neck. Khale tucked either end of it into the drawstring of his pants. There was nothing to be done for those, of course; fashioning pants from what was left of the curtains would consume too much time. Perhaps they would be lucky, and everyone in the village would be idiots?

"What do you want to see once you leave here?" Khale asked. He took the knife from Konrad's hand and set to work on Konrad's appearance.

"Animals," Konrad thought. Not to see, but to eat, to taste the meat... "Food. Women and children. A new landscape. What about you?"

"Quality food would be nice," he speculated, "even if it's just wild-caught. Something we haven't eaten before. A new landscape. New weather."

"New weather," Konrad agreed. "And venison." He studied Khale's serious, so-changed countenance as he worked at making Konrad appear healthy and cared-for. "A farm, perhaps?" he suggested. "Weston could find us a place."

"A farm," Khale agreed. He took the longest middle section of Konrad's beard in his hands and swept it away with a precise and deliberate motion. Despite the care Khale took, it still hurt; the roots were unused to that sort of pressure.

Konrad reminded himself that the blade had dulled quickly as he'd worked his way through Khale's hair. It was probably more painful for Konrad than it had been for Khale.

"With livestock and a dog," Khale suggested. He pressed his lips to Konrad's briefly, still tense. When he pulled away, he crossed to the window and made a curtain-vest like his own for Konrad to wear.

With their sleeves rolled up, they looked almost civilized again, Konrad mused as he tucked the curtain into his pants.

"To the bay?" he suggested. "Then to our farm."

"With a boy, a necklace, and some medicine," Konrad agreed. It was an immeasurable risk, but the payout, if they succeeded, was priceless. "You look so different trimmed," Konrad told him. "We may just manage this."

Khale put on an unnaturally deep voice: "Does this help?" he teased.

Konrad laughed, caught in the warmth of the moment amidst this fear. He kissed him, deeper and bittersweet. "Nothing could improve you," he said.

Tears sprung to Khale's eyes; each of them knew this would be one of their last kisses. He pulled away, his voice gruff as he suggested, "We could name our dog Roshank."

"If you like," Konrad murmured. He was out of excuses to keep Khale in this room. "That's a good name."

"I do," Khale said, and surprised him with another kiss. He ran his hand along Konrad's hairline and then through to the back of his neck. "You look good. Fresh to the island, young."

Konrad kissed him again. One last time. "Whatever happens," he asserted, "we push to the bay."

"Whatever happens," Khale countered, "you survive."

"That's my line," Konrad teased. They held hands and approached the window, the escape, seeking freedom or death.

23

WESTON

Weston knew one thing with absolute certainty: Going back to the Stilts would not help. It was the wrong move. He had to stay on the main side of the island. The currents of ideas worked their way through his mind: *How do I stay here? How do I get back to Konrad and Khale?*

His solution began with his hand dancing across the barbed edges of the stitches that held his back together. He pulled at them, gently at first to hide his expressions, then all at once while no one was watching.

He used the pain to cough, which in the end didn't sound worse than any other cough he had had since becoming ill. He hoped it would be impactful enough.

"Deyton," he pleaded, his voice raspy.

Then he fell.

He hoped to collapse to the ground as though he had fainted. However, his desire to not hurt himself too much made it more of an awkward collapse onto his knees, then his hands, and finally his side.

Deyton bolted to his side, lifting him off the ground. "Come on."

He lifted Weston all the way into his arms and left the building.

To Weston's relief, they headed south, away from the Stilts and the gold mines.

"Why didn't you say anything?" Deyton asked.

Weston let his body hang limp for a moment, his eyes still open. He took slow and deliberate breaths. "I thought..." he began. He coughed. His back burned, the pain increased by the second. He felt the wetness of blood as it saturated what he had left of his shirt. He didn't want to look at his shirt and see what the past few days had done to it.

"I thought I was okay," he spat out. He let his head loll backwards, looking at the earth behind them as Deyton carried him through the village.

"You're bleeding!" Deyton exclaimed. His hand moved away from the clotted fabric. "Why? Did you hurt yourself when you fell?"

"I had the fluid drained before the trial. My stitches must have broken," Weston replied.

Deyton opened a door to his own room and set Weston down on the bed. "Let me see."

Weston rolled onto his stomach to expose the hole in his back. He tried to raise his arms, and the pain was too much. He let them rest halfway up his back. In an endless ache, he hoped Deyton would have the heart to heal.

"This was the second one," Weston added.

Deyton examined his back for a moment. He did the percussion taps again then felt his head.

"You need the medicine we have," Deyton said.

Yes, but they won't give it to me.

Deyton helped Weston sit up. "Why hasn't anyone given it to you?"

"I wasn't allowed to have it. It's expensive and in limited supply," Weston replied, mocking Ambrose in a childish tone.

There was gold sitting in the mountains, hardly covered by dirt, and Ambrose was convincing the people there wasn't enough currency to buy—or make—a small amount of mold. He hated the tedium of the island.

Deyton's brows turned down. The inner corners of his eyes, nose, and mouth scrunched together. He looked at Weston and then out the window behind the bed, "What crime has earned you that punishment?"

Weston cleared his throat; now was the time to prove, to their most influential people, how wrong everything was there—how unjust their system was.

Except clearing his throat sent him into a coughing fit. Deyton supported him until his body stilled.

"I washed up on the wrong side of the island," he told Deyton. At the heart of everything he had been through, it came down to that one key fact.

Though he knew he hadn't actually washed up on the wrong side. He had washed up exactly where he was meant to.

"Can I trust you to wait here while I get the medicine you need?" Deyton asked. "You need some on the wound and some to eat."

Weston looked up at him. "Where am I going to go?"

Not that he was incapable of walking or incapable of leaving the room; there was a window. He could find his way out. The problem was that everyone in the town would notice him and would know who he was.

The other problem was that he was trying to trust his instincts, and Luck wanted him to get medicine *before* trying anything else.

It sent a shiver through his spine; he felt how close to death he was, despite having all his mind available to him. He would have thought himself closer when he had been delirious.

Deyton huffed, a smile dancing across his tight-pulled lips. "I almost believe your innocence."

He left the room.

Like a good little Luck fairy, Weston waited. He made himself lie on his stomach, even though it was difficult to breathe, and focused on the way his body moved with each breath.

It took Deyton one hundred and eighty-six breaths to return. Weston had turned mid-count, so he could see the door when Deyton came in.

Deyton paused at the entryway and assessed Weston. He entered the space. He hung his jacket over the edge of a chair and removed his shoes.

Weston missed his shoes; he had worn none in days. If he could bend over, he suspected he would see calluses and crust encasing his dirty soles.

Deyton moved beside him, and Weston assumed the position: chest to the bed, teeth bared, fists clenched. He knew it wouldn't hurt as much, but he was ready for an intense stinging sensation.

"This may hurt a bit," Deyton warned him.

Weston felt ice cold cream pressed into his incision. Deyton dotted it around the wound, pushing lightly but moving slowly to ensure full coverage.

"Who are you?" Deyton asked.

"Weston Akhan," he said. Then he shook his head against the table. "I am James Nukoin, Prince of Wyvern. But to the world, he is dead. I will never be James again. But I will be king someday."

"Not if we don't see you home." Deyton placed a bandage over the wound and affixed it with gauze around Weston's chest. Next, he handed Weston a cup. "Drink," he insisted.

Weston gazed into the cup. He closed his eyes and gulped it, a bitter taste that demanded he heave it back up consumed his senses. He forced it down, which took all of his remaining will.

When he looked back up, he faced Deyton's brown and pepper hair that made him look just old enough to be wise but young enough to be capable of more than Ambrose.

"Some men in this place lose sight of our mission here," Deyton said. He handed Weston a beige shirt.

Deyton helped him remove the rest of his shirt and put the new one on. He also handed him a pair of pants. Thankfully, he made Weston put those on himself. While Weston sorted how to dress with minimal pain, Deyton turned to rinse his hands in a basin of water atop a small chest of drawers.

"What is your mission? To be keepers of knowledge?" Weston asked.

"And to serve Maelchor. I don't see how punishing you for nothing is serving anyone unless there's a god of spite."

Weston chuckled, pain cutting through his body. He certainly felt like there was a god of spite.

Deyton turned back to face him. "I need to see Ambrose again while you rest. He's made a mistake."

Perhaps. But my time here is coming to an end.

"Your curse isn't a curse," Weston told him as he left the room.

"Isn't it?" Deyton asked, his hand pulling the door shut.

"Wait!" Weston called out.

Deyton took a step back inside the room. "Yes?"

Weston felt the possibilities of their magic and tried to sort out what they meant. It wasn't a time for reflection, but it mattered. He had heard the stories growing up, about Delkies and their nature, Gancanagh and their curse. He knew the Selkies were as dark, if not darker, than the Gancanagh.

"It isn't meant to be a curse," Weston said. "It forces the Selkies to reproduce. They don't want to. It's supposed to save your race."

"I can see that, if one Selkie is bound to me," he replied. "But how many Selkies can one man save from this?"

Deyton shook his head again and then nodded toward Weston. "Come with me."

Weston got up, following Luck.

Weston could sense the conviction in Deyton's voice, how unwilling he was to accept that somewhere others did not see him as a castaway, that he could have had a different life. As they walked between wooden houses and through the village, Weston noticed the ways their lifestyle had been shaped to their commitment, their purpose: nearly a thousand castaway men, all convicted of murder because of the curse, living in harmony.

Something was missing: If the curse wasn't designed to hurt women and each man could only handle so many...

It was about attachment. Perhaps even a lie. Did the Gancanagh curse *every* woman they saw? Or did they only curse one...a mate?

He doubted anyone was willing to experiment.

"If the whole of your race were paired," he mused to Deyton. "It wouldn't kill anyone. One man. One woman."

It would also limit the Selkies, and that was where legend said the curse originated from: They didn't want to settle down. They wanted more freedom. More freedom was costing them their entire race.

"The intakes have slowed," Weston pointed out. "Because no one is breeding, not because the gene has been erased."

"That may be, but I see no way to turn that tide. If we went to shore, we'd face angry mothers and husbands of women who fell prey to the curse. More would die. We need a way to limit the effects of the curse."

Weston sighed as they rounded another corner. He could have taken them to Ambrose, but he didn't want to unveil his magic. Instead, he let Deyton lead them through the village.

He wasn't sure what to think of the curse. There had to be some way to help the Gancanagh be free, but they had all killed someone (through their curse, but it was still murder). They would never be welcomed back. The men there, the men already alive, had little hope.

"There's a cure," Weston said, the feeling bubbling to his lips before he could stop himself.

There was a cure somewhere, but he didn't know what it was. It was a secret, hidden from most.

He didn't know why he was telling Deyton this.

"There may be," Deyton replied, his hand falling in three hard knocks against a door.

"When I find it," Weston said, careful to feel the ebbing of his magic as it aligned with his idea. "I'll hire you at my school. To teach children."

Deyton laughed, but Weston knew the ability to pass on his knowledge—his legacy—had tempted him.

They didn't speak anymore. Within a moment, the large wooden door in front of them opened. Ambrose was there. "What has happened? You should be in the foothills by now."

"The boy was ill," Deyton replied.

It was an optimistic claim Weston wasn't ready to take as fact; he was better, but not *no-longer ill.*

"Yes," Ambrose stated, hurried and annoyed. "He was ill an hour ago when you set out."

Weston hated the man and how little he cared about Weston's fate. So desperate to keep his hands clean of his moral plunders, he'd missed the chance to kill Weston when he could have, when a simple slip would have been understandable. Or, perhaps Luck had warred against him during the operation, and he had lost.

Hands be damned, their blood would stain his soul.

Air sucked into Weston's chest, and he let it tickle and burn until it burst forth in a violent spat of coughs.

Deyton set his hand against Weston's back as he coughed and then on his shoulder after. "I think someone has set himself against the boy."

Ambrose looked outside, then he opened the door wider. "Come in. Let me hear you out."

He sounded reasonable, reasonable and caring, and like the leader he should have been. Weston couldn't figure him out.

To burden himself with the limitations of his beliefs was to go against his own nature.

Deyton waited for Weston to enter, and so he did. Ambrose entered last and shut the door, sealing them inside.

Ambrose moved to a chair and sat. Weston heard the creak of his bones like rusted hinges. "Tell me what you think is going on," he asked them.

He asked *Deyton.* Without his magic, Weston would have gone off on Ambrose. With it, he relaxed and let Deyton handle the confrontation. It would mean more to Ambrose, coming from someone he respected and not a child.

As Deyton spoke, he paced the room. The wooden planks were aligned just right for the stride.

"He has no reason to be here; he's committed no crime. Someone wants him in the Stilts without medicine to cure him. There's no reason for it," Deyton explained.

Ambrose leaned back in his chair, rubbing his hand through his beard. "Isn't there? He's not one of us, just as the men in the Stilts are different."

"He's not even fifty," Deyton insisted.

"But he is an adult," Ambrose pointed out.

Barely. Ambrose used the same logic his father used: adult enough to be murdered.

Ambrose watched Weston fight back the urge to point this out and then folded his arms. "I'm relieved to see that your compassion has you defending the boy, Deyton. Did you give him medicine?"

Between Deyton's brows furrowing and his pace ending, Weston wasn't sure who was winning. "I did, yes. Ointment and the bitter drink."

Weston glanced between the two men and then pleaded to Ambrose, "Death shouldn't be a punishment for being different."

Deyton nodded.

"I have long thought that," Ambrose said to Weston. He unfolded his arms and set them on the edges of his armchair. "Tell me how this boy differs from the men we've sentenced to the Stilts. Make a case for his freedom."

There was silence.

Uh oh.

Weston was going to die because Deyton didn't have a case for his freedom, for his life, for anything.

He just had the ability to agree with things.

Weston's gut twisted inside.

After the painstaking silence, Deyton spoke. "I..."

Weston was going to die.

Finally, Deyton spoke a full sentence. "He seems to be innocent of any wrongdoing."

His whole life came down to the fact that nothing had been about his wrongdoing, but it was the reason he should be free.

He shouldn't have been *sentenced* if that logic was going to apply to the situation.

Ambrose stood and walked toward a window.

"You disappoint me, Deyton. I asked for differences, not simi-larities."

Weston felt sick.

"He's young," Deyton provided.

"Magne and Casek are only a few years older."

"Then there are no differences, aside from the obvious."

Weston was fuming and nauseated and coughing again. All progress Weston had made with Deyton would be gone; Deyton would keep punishing the gay Gancanagh for no reason.

"Is that a crime?" Ambrose asked, pushing, seeking the resolution that would seal Deyton as Weston's enemy.

"It seems to be one," Deyton stated, slowly and carefully. "If it weren't, why would they punish them?"

"Why was the boy punished?" Ambrose prodded.

Deyton looked at Weston and studied him. Weston tried to look dying and innocent.

He *was* dying and innocent.

"Spite?" Deyton asked.

At least he sounded confused. Weston felt a surge of energy.

Deyton sifted through his thoughts aloud. "You mean the men of the Stilts have no reason to be punished."

"Yes. I used Weston as a means to see if anyone might wake to the injustice of the arrangement." Ambrose pulled something out of his pocket—a key—and handed it to Deyton. "I'm retiring. You'll replace me as head of the council."

Weston stood. He was, as it happened, standing to begin with, but he stood more. "When my people find out my fate, you'll bring war to these islands," he lied liberally. "Just for mistreating a boy."

"What fate?" Ambrose asked, smug and calculating. "You have your medicine. You'll have your boat and your escort."

Weston moved closer, so he was looking up at Ambrose. "That I was treated in spite, despite being helpless. By you. By the men in the Stilts. By that *pedophile*."

Weston may have been an adult, but Luck said younger men had passed through and become his victims. Weston wasn't the first he'd attempted to touch.

Ambrose smiled. "You were used as a symbol to save the ones you have come to know as friends."

Air forced his lungs full again, his body ready to lunge. It still hurt, but he was too angry to care.

Then Ambrose's words sunk in—a symbol to *save.*

Ambrose was helping him.

"Oh," Weston said, deflated and in pain and coughing. He sat. *What?*

"Your friends will have better lives now," Ambrose said. "Yes?"

Deyton kneeled in front of Weston's hunched-over body. "Yes, I think so." Deyton then rose to his feet and turned away from Weston. "We have empty houses on the east side of the village."

Ambrose extended his hand to Weston. "Come along. I have a boat ready."

Oh.

Luck was wrong. Or confused. He was confused.

"Thank you," Weston said, more to Deyton than to Ambrose.

For Ambrose, he offered, "I don't understand." Then he took Ambrose's hand, and they walked out the door, Deyton at their heels.

"Ask whatever you need," Ambrose said. His arm wrapped around Weston's shoulders.

"Why couldn't you be decent?" Weston asked, accusing, demanding, frustrated.

"It was a gamble. I had to be sure of Deyton's understanding. It still won't be an easy transition, but Konrad and Khale will be safe now. You did that for them."

"I did?"

Weston looked out at the world: the village and the ocean beyond. They would be free. Their freedom had come at a cost, as had Weston's life. It was a price Weston had seen no alternative but to pay. Was that Luck? Perhaps. Was it right? Weston hoped so.

He had so much to learn—about himself, about Luck. He couldn't take on his family like this.

He searched his feelings, the ones he didn't trust deeply, for a hint of deception from Ambrose.

His instincts about Ambrose realigned. Luck had changed its opinion with experience, which meant all of the feelings he had, his instincts, were based on experience.

That left infinite room for error.

He'd journeyed this far only to rediscover what he'd found on the sinking ship: Luck was a bastard pretending to be his best friend.

Even the boat was prepared. Khale...

Weston could see a future where Khale survived. Without Ambrose against them, possibilities unfolded. Khale's potential was growing, glowing, and present.

"Do you see?" Ambrose asked, almost as though he knew of Weston's magic.

He did see it, and he felt it too: the tide changing, hope.

Ambrose put his hand on Weston's upper back. "You committed no crime, and Deyton recognized this to be the case. He understood the corollary between you and the men of the Stilts—that they have done no more wrong than you. He learned to see the injustice there; others will. He has a strong network of supporters in the village."

Back in Wyvern, Weston had no one.

How could he expect to lead if he didn't have the people?

Weston squared his shoulders. "I need to leave with Konrad. He's been enlisted to serve. The frontlines."

A burst of laughter, short and small and quiet, erupted from Ambrose. "What is it you do that has him listening to you?"

He would tell Ambrose soon, but right now he was irritated by his own miscalculation—his misbelief that Ambrose was bad.

"I have a strong conviction about my life," Weston summarized.

"So has he."

They continued walking toward the pier—Weston more determined than ever to get Konrad and Khale off the island. He was sorting through the island's future and Deyton's role in it. He searched weather patterns and projections. His mind was racing, ready for the next step.

"You'll let us go?" Weston asked.

Ambrose nodded. "The tides brought more than a young man to our shores."

This was it. This was his beginning. He'd lost everything he thought was his life, including his regard for his father, his home, and his name. He might never see his mother again. But, he had allies now. Not just Konrad and Khale; he had Deyton and the Gancanagh. Their age and experience in surviving something difficult would be useful. Weston could grow and learn under their eyes.

He wasn't alone. He wasn't on the wrong island. This place forged warriors. He'd survived pain—even being told he could not have medicine constructed a will to live in Weston. Yes, he'd needed the medicine, but he suspected Ambrose knew what he was doing.

He *hoped* Ambrose knew what he was doing. Otherwise, it was down to Luck. And as far as Luck went, he did not know Luck very well. He needed to explore it, to learn the limitations and nuances within himself, to create an alliance within himself, between what he knew of the world and what Luck could share.

Weston was brimming. He'd emerged, sort of. There was still the issue of getting off the island, but he felt the path forward, and the obstructions had been cut back.

He had a future. He had tools. He had access to gold, and he had friends who were cunning warriors and strategists.

For the first time in days, he realized he'd been surviving with little hope. As the pieces fell into place with their footsteps, his heart shifted: he had hope.

Weston breathed. The medication was working slowly but surely. He could see again. It must have been more than mere mold — spelled with a foreign magic to encourage healing.

The group passed by a man. Something familiar tugged at Weston. Luck demanded he look closer. They were moving slowly, but not slow enough. The man had short blonde hair and a clean shaved face. His eyes were green and he wore fresh clothes.

Weston blinked. He was out of place. He nearly missed a step, catching himself before he tumbled across the ground. The man was gone.

He'd missed something else. Something huge.

The man he had been was a body they'd sent to sea.

Why had there been a fire fae on the island?

How is he still alive?

Why does he look identical to my uncle?

Ambrose helped Weston stand. "Are you alright?"

"I...don't know."

24

KONRAD

Moving through the village alone, with no escort aside from Khale, with the illusion of being a free man, Konrad saw the place in a new way. He saw the appeal, so frustrating in his youth, of a community that worked together to keep the village sturdy and clean. He imagined millennia of men working towards the same outcomes, the history and camaraderie of the place.

Those things had been lost on him in his youth, but he saw them now in his way, and a part of him was surprised to find that he longed for them.

He identified it after a moment of thought: What he really longed for was a home, safe and secure, with Khale. Not the home they'd had, not the struggle for survival. He wanted the farm and the dog Khale wanted. Roshank—the name he wanted for the dog—meant *friend*, and Khale deserved many friends.

A chasm separated him from Khale's touch, from the connection he longed to feel. The air between them was charged with tension and longing. Konrad offered Khale a small smile of shared sentiment.

Just as he looked forward again, someone appeared from around the corner of a building ahead of them. It was Florian of all people—

the man who'd accused them of hurting Weston, who'd spread lies about him in the village to prevent his rescue.

He gave them a welcoming smile. "Hallo," he said. "I didn't know they'd sent new people on the last boat."

Konrad saw Khale's back tighten. "Hello," he said carefully.

"You're a bit old to be new, aren't you?" Florian asked. His tone didn't have a suspicious edge; it was only curious.

Konrad recalled Khale's deeper voice and changed his own, altering the lilt which was particular to himself. "We were in hiding," he explained. "There was a group of us down along the point."

Most continents had a peninsula somewhere, he supposed. It was the easiest isolated land feature to be sure existed.

"Have you eaten?" Florian asked.

They had not. He would have liked to go with Florian and get himself and Khale some sort of hearty meal, but he knew it would have made them sick. They had their sights on a greater prize anyway.

"We have," Khale lied. "Everyone is very generous here. How long have you lived here?"

"Decades," Florian complained. "Too long." He looked back toward the village and then turned his neatly trimmed face back toward them. "We've a group that plays cards in the evening, if you'd like to join. Down at the old hub."

If Konrad had more time, he would have liked to go. To sit at a table and study Florian and his network in the community until he had the means to completely undercut his reputational standing among the villagers. To hurt him, as he'd done to Weston.

Vengeance took time and energy Konrad was unwilling to expend on such a purposeless cause.

"We will see you there," Khale assured him. They walked away.

"Enjoy the afternoon!" Florian called after them.

Konrad breathed again once they'd turned the nearest corner and found themselves on an isolated side path between the wall of a house and a copse of thin, stunted trees.

"The hair worked," Khale marveled. He looked like he might

want to kiss Konrad, but in place of that, each of them took a step apart, widening the distance between them.

Konrad shook his head, angered by the encounter. It should have been nothing more than a relief, but to know Florian would continue to thrive here... "He's as shallow as low tide," Konrad muttered.

"Will you promise me something?" Khale asked. They fell into step together, their pace more deliberate after the encounter. The bay represented safety. They needed to get there; they could flee into the water if they had to. Weston would come to them by boat.

"So long as it doesn't involve leaving you," Konrad teased in a low voice. "Yes."

That elicited a laugh from Khale, which made Konrad smile despite himself. Whatever their situation, they would be themselves throughout.

"That you will try, every day you're off this island, to be optimistic once," Khale said. "Even if it's that your shit won't wash back up to your front step."

Konrad laughed too.

"Alright," he agreed. "Will you promise me something in return?"

Khale's voice tightened but still bore the undertones of teasing. "Everyone dies, Konrad."

Yes, but not everyone suffered for decades first.

He allowed himself a frown, and then he refocused. "That you will try every day you're off this island, wherever you are, to do something new and trust that it will be alright."

"Alright," Khale mimicked with a small smile.

They stood on the edge of a shallow ravine, which ran the remainder of the way toward the bay and the pier that jutted out from the shore. On the opposite bank, cresting the hill beyond, Weston appeared. Beside him, Ambrose walked with an arm around Weston's shoulder.

"He won't fall for the hair," Konrad realized aloud. They'd likely already been recognized. "Hide or face them?"

Khale set his jaw. "Face them."

Konrad reached for his hand—there was no use in denying it now —and smiled again. "Alright," he said.

They crossed the ravine in silence, hand-in-hand, and scaled the shallow wall beyond.

"What is the purpose," Ambrose asked in a friendlier tone than Konrad had heard in days, "of locking doors in a room with windows?" He smiled at Konrad before casting a less self-assured gaze on Khale.

"We would have found another way out," Konrad stated, because it was true and so that he might afford himself some time to assess Weston.

Weston was waxen, drawn from his days of suffering, but his posture beside Ambrose lacked the tension Konrad expected.

"Where are you two going?" Weston asked.

"An excursion around the bay," Konrad said. It was perhaps one of the more pointless conversations of his life. They could talk niceties and ignore the palpable threat that one of them posed to the other three. "Where are you off to?"

"Weston has the necklace," Ambrose said in a clipped voice. "I'm escorting him home."

Khale straightened. The Stilts were not Weston's home. "They'll hurt him," he argued.

"Maybe you should come too, then," Weston suggested. He had a light in his eyes Konrad hadn't seen since that first morning when they'd extricated him from the vines.

"Why will they hurt Weston?" Ambrose asked.

Khale hesitated. He glanced at Konrad. Something was off. "The Stilts are the other way...where are you going?"

"*Home*," Weston said with enough emphasis to cause him to cough.

Konrad struggled to sort the pieces into a reality that made sense. What would motivate Ambrose to behave as he had and then change his tune now after so much fear?

Perhaps Weston had swayed him in some way, using his intuitive magic.

Ambrose laughed. "You have too little faith in me," he said warmly. "I've resigned; Deyton oversees the council. Would you prefer to come with us or stay?"

Ambrose ought to stay, to ease the transition. Deyton seemed like a decent enough sort, but like any new leader he would benefit from the aid of his predecessor.

"With us?" Weston asked. Konrad could see he hadn't known the old man's intent.

It seemed none of them had.

"I'd like to see another place before I die," Ambrose explained. "Even just for a moment. That is my price to get you off this island."

What would it serve, besides the man's own selfishness? Konrad glanced at Khale, wary of Weston's apparent trust.

He wanted to trust Ambrose too. A thousand years of friendship drove him toward the trust, but a thousand years of hunger drove him to doubt. "I'm not certain," he murmured. Khale didn't seem to be either. Konrad looked at Weston. "Will you tell us what is going on?"

"We're leaving the island," Weston stated. His eyes settled on Khale. "All of us."

"Are you compelled to leave, or do you do so of your own volition?" Konrad clarified. Leaving with Weston still at risk wouldn't be acceptable to Khale.

Konrad would kill Ambrose if he had to.

He waited for Weston's response, tense, hand on the knife.

"It's a good thing," Weston insisted.

"You are joining us?" Khale asked Ambrose after a laugh. "Escaping the island? *You*?"

Ambrose raised his head, dignified. "I like to think of it as relieving them of our presence more than escaping. I try not to break laws."

Khale laughed again, at the same moment that Weston urged, "We need to move."

A moment later, over the edge of the ravine, a crowd of men appeared.

Konrad gauged the distance to the water. They could run if

needed—with or without Ambrose. He wondered whether he might be successful in outrunning that group of men while carrying Ambrose.

His doubts ran high.

One man broke away from the main body of the group and began the descent toward their position in the ravine, the pier only steps away.

Deyton, the friendly guard, broke away as well and stood defensively between their group and the stray man. "They have permission to go," he told the man, loudly enough for his voice to carry to the men on the ridge. "They'll be back," he added.

Ambrose stepped beside Deyton with that steady, humble way he had. He spoke in his same gentle voice. There would be a dispute over what he had said. "I've passed my role as head of the council on to Deyton," he explained to the stray man.

Konrad's every instinct urged him away from this situation. This was wrong; Ambrose ought to stay long enough to see Deyton established. This was on the verge of becoming a mob, and Konrad wanted nothing more than to get Khale off this island intact.

They were too unbearably close to freedom to lose him now.

He began, hand on Khale's, to back slowly away from Ambrose.

Weston stepped forward. "They're sending me home because no one likes me."

Several of the men on the ridge nodded in agreement. Nothing could unite them, save the thread of a common enemy.

"He's a prince," Deyton added. Konrad arched his eyebrows and wondered what, precisely, Weston had shared with the man. "We can't keep him here."

"So, send him alone!" someone from the ridge bellowed.

The men from the ridge, first one, then another, then more, began the descent toward them.

Konrad squeezed Khale's hand. Any moment now, they would need to run.

"I can't navigate or do the work," Weston explained. "I need their strength."

"What strength?" the man nearest them scoffed, eyes on Ambrose.

Still with his same confidence, Ambrose reminded the man, "I'm the one of our company who knows the stars. I'm old. They're banished from the village. If someone must be killed for leaving the island, isn't it better that it's us, not you?"

"If you're going to be killed," the man said. He pointed toward the necklace, which Ambrose wore around his neck.

Khale squeezed Konrad's hand.

"Why are you going back on their sentences?" One man from the ridge asked. He was now only a man's height away.

Ambrose put his hand on Deyton's shoulder. "He'll explain. Better than I will."

He'd likely be killed, along with them, the way this talk was going.

Deyton began his explanation, and while he spoke, Ambrose turned and looked at Konrad and Khale. "Let's go," he said.

The four of them turned away from the crowd of men. It was, perhaps, the most dangerous thing any of them had ever done, to turn their back on an enemy, but they walked together.

Before them, the pier stretched like a road into the sunset-molten water.

25

WESTON

The pier was much like the Stilts in construction. Weston liked the way the waves rolled under the pillars of the dock, crashing against wood and rocky shore. In key ways, the pier was not like the Stilts: The wood was newer and free of obvious signs of wear. The men of the village clearly treated it against weather and replaced parts as needed. A small boat hovered beside it, bobbing with the waves.

They were almost ready to set out, to be free of the island, but Luck itched at Weston's senses. He couldn't leave now, not yet. He looked back toward the village to think. Somewhere out there was the answer. Was it his uncle? No... He just had to track down the thought and follow it until he knew.

He couldn't follow his whims. The Gancanagh were already upset with them. They had to leave *now*.

Luck rallied against Weston's convictions as he boarded the small boat.

The heavy humid air clung to Weston's skin and the sea mist left droplets on everything Weston watched the rain leaving the clouds like wisps being pulled from their billowing form in the distance.

He bounced from foot to foot. *What is it?*

It wasn't something at the Stilts, but it had to do with the Stilts. Their fate, he thought. Yes, something about their fate.

They would have better housing soon, according to Deyton.

He wondered if it was Deyton who was causing the issue, but again, that wasn't it. He felt himself getting closer, though...Deyton. It centered around Deyton

Weston looked at the crowd gathering near the pier, held at bay by Deyton and his new ideas. They were good ideas, but they were unwelcome to the ears of the village.

"Deyton needs to come with us," Weston declared.

He would never make progress on the islands.

Konrad stood straighter from his hunched-over position and looked at Weston and then to Ambrose. "I'll go."

"Tell him they won't listen, and he will die if he stays," Weston requested of Konrad.

Though he had a bond with Konrad and Khale, Weston had also connected with Deyton in a way he would never forget. He wanted the man safe if his efforts would be useless here. He had talents the world could benefit from.

"Would you like to come with us?" Konrad yelled to Deyton. "You may know which thing is best to say."

Weston set down the rope he was bundling. He reached for the sides of the pier to steady himself, the small vessel rocking as he moved. Khale offered his hand to aid Weston.

Weston took the steps, bridging the gap between the boat and the dock. "Okay."

The two of them walked at a fast pace, forcing Weston to push his lungs past their comfort zone. He coughed, and Konrad slowed.

In a winded exhale, Weston called out to the man.

Deyton turned toward them and then took a step away from the angry, growing crowd. "You should go before they stop you."

"You need to come with us. You'll die here," Weston said.

"I appreciate your concern, but I think I have this well in hand. They just need some persuasion."

If persuasion included a few barrels of alcohol and some herbs Weston had been told to never eat, then yes, they needed persuasion.

"They won't respond to it," Weston insisted. "If you want to live...." He should have told Deyton about his magic sooner, when it would have made a difference to this conversation. Now, it would look like a convenient way to excuse his desire to rescue Deyton.

Deyton was too strong-headed a man, too dedicated to his vision for the men of the island, to listen.

"Please," Weston begged.

Konrad stepped forward, looking directly at Deyton for the first time, instead of the crowd. "The boy has a unique magic, similar to the ascended Selkies."

"This is where Maelchor has asked me to serve," Deyton replied. He spoke with a calm conviction Weston knew wouldn't sway; only his desire to keep Deyton alive had brought them back into the mob. He needed to let it go, to return to the boat.

He had to try, too. His conscience would not let him go without trying.

"What if he sent us to save you?" Konrad asked.

Yes, that might work.

"So you could serve elsewhere," Weston added. "To greater effect. You grew your skill here. Now you're needed elsewhere."

Deyton pulled the key out from his pocket as evidence. "I'm needed here. I must help these men see the wrongness of their thinking."

More than before, Weston knew it was useless to continue pushing Deyton.

He let the air escape his body in a *humph* of frustration.

"They won't; but you will never be forgotten. Your work is not useless," Weston told him—solace for a dying man, he hoped.

The problem with Luck, in seeing the chance of something happening, was that if you went against it the guilt was more. He didn't want Deyton to have his last thoughts be full of regret for not leaving. Weston had followed his convictions and done his best.

Weston wouldn't forget him, not across all the seas or a lifetime of years.

"I will coax them toward it. They're angry now, but some food and a warm fire should help them," Deyton insisted.

Konrad looked at Weston; Weston looked at Konrad.

"Let's go," Weston said. "We've saved Khale for the day."

Konrad stepped closer to Deyton and hugged him.

Weston tried not to react. Deyton would lose respect for being compassionate toward them. He would lose his place in society for helping them and for allowing them to leave. They did not only banish those who were gay, but those who were friends of them too.

His fate was dismal.

Weston watched as Konrad whispered something to Deyton, but he couldn't hear what it was. When he was done, Konrad stepped back and looked toward Weston again. "Alright."

"Tell Ambrose I won't let him down," Deyton said.

Deyton returned to the group, and Weston took off toward the pier with Konrad.

"Does he have any hope?" Konrad asked.

"He has 'til night," Weston replied, a frown spreading from his face through his soul. Before, they had days to accept they couldn't help Khale and exhaust all options he saw. Within that time, the tide had changed. Deyton had entered his life as quickly as he was leaving it with no room for aid. The good he could have done for the island would be lost along with his life.

"Let's get Khale out of here," Konrad declared.

"Yeah, sure. This was never about me," Weston joked.

He wasn't going home to Wyvern, but he would be home with his new family, wherever the sea carried them. To Paisca, South of Angmaan, he hoped. It was close enough for trade but far enough for seclusion.

"Let's get him out of here," Weston agreed.

26

KONRAD

Ambrose had been more than prepared for this moment: He'd stocked the boat with crates, though most were disorganized. Konrad slid the last of the box crates under the prow of the little boat. They'd be taking it north and east along the shore to where Weston and Ambrose assured them a felucca waited.

Konrad worried the sails would be rotted, but Ambrose had smiled placidly when he'd voiced his concerns. He chose to scowl at the crates they loaded, rather than at Ambrose. He still didn't understand when or why the situation with Ambrose had changed.

Like so much of their time with Weston, it came down to trust.

He patted the last of the crates with a smile at Khale. "Weston insists this has something besides salted fish in it, but I'm skeptical."

Khale laughed as he pushed the boat from the pier, but his thoughts were interrupted as his gaze caught Ambrose, eyes cast on the island. Khale met Konrad's eyes and whispered quietly, "He's a good man."

Whatever qualities Ambrose possessed, tired topped the list.

"We tried," Weston told him. The old man and the young man sat opposite each other on separate woven seats. An intangible understanding occupied the space between them. "You're a good man too."

Khale swung his lean body over the side of the dory, splashing water over the interior of the boat.

"We made it off the island," he marveled. He took the seat at the stern, where there was space for both him and Konrad to sit across, and Konrad draped his hand across Khale's lower back and kissed him.

"With the most precious cargo," he agreed. He tugged at Khale's shortened beard, a lightness in his heart that his body had long forgotten. "And trimmed hair."

"And," Khale teased with his own tug of Konrad's beard, "you managed to save Weston."

"Who?" Konrad joked.

Ambrose looked at the pair of them with a smile of his own. Only Weston's face was shadowed, turned away from them in the sunset.

"When we arrive," Ambrose instructed. "We can establish ourselves as a family: grandfather, sons, grandson. So long as we're careful, we should be safe."

Weston spoke from his silhouette: "I have an intuition magic. If I practice, I can ensure everyone is safe."

Ambrose was skilled in a deceitful manner of seeming vague and old and perhaps a bit distracted, but now, he turned sharp raven eyes on Konrad as his understanding of the situation shifted. "Is that how you managed all of this?" he commented. He'd rediscovered that same tone he used all those years of mentoring Konrad.

Konrad was unconvinced. He flicked his eyes toward Weston. "He managed it. We only listened and trusted."

Faith in Maelchor was about the old ways, tradition, and upholding values that had served the world for generations. Faith in Weston was about evidence, trust, and miracles that worked in the span of a few days. Faith in Ambrose would have to be re-forged, if it could be salvaged at all, and was about old friendships and truths that went beyond romance or family. They were down to understanding.

Faith in Khale was about giving half of his self to be carried around by another. It was about hours of mutual silence, words spoken and unspoken, letting the most important portion of himself belong to Khale, and trusting Khale with it. It was about carrying half of Khale inside himself so that regardless of either of their fates both would live.

The Gancanagh of the island were meant to be men of faith, serving Maelchor for all their lives.

Leaving the island now, Konrad knew he was a man of faith—in his boatmates and perhaps, most importantly, in himself. That was a new sort of faith. He was unsure what to do with it, aside from marvel that he possessed it.

He could use it, he supposed, to protect his three companions.

Ambrose shifted seats, disturbing Konrad's thoughts. "Can you forgive me?" Ambrose asked Weston. He must have coughed again, Konrad thought; he hadn't listened.

He straightened and addressed Weston. "Before you answer him...what happened to Tomlin? The man who found us on the mountain?" Konrad wasn't convinced, after the way he'd behaved, that Tomlin was his true name.

"We fashioned a shipping crate into a cell for him," Ambrose assured Konrad. His voice carried emotions Konrad felt toward Tomlin: that there were lines one should not cross and that Tomlin's desires concerning Weston crossed them. "He'll live there for ten years."

"He won't live that long," Weston said as he stood and joined Ambrose on the bow seat so that he could see Konrad and Khale. "They'll kill him for being involved."

An ironic sort of justice in a way.

Too many had died this week. Khale and Weston had nearly been among them.

"What of the men in the Stilts?" Konrad asked.

Weston shrugged one shoulder. "It depends."

"They live for the time being?" Konrad pressed. He wanted to imagine that they thrived, though he knew that would not be the case. Cruelty would continue if Deyton met his end.

The weight of his quest settled on him then: find a way to cure the curse, a means of giving every man on the island something similar to the necklace so that each man might go his own way.

"Most of them," Weston said after a moment of concentration. The boat rocked over the crest of a larger wave. "It's a harsh winter."

Konrad decided not to ask names, faces. If he never knew which died, they could all be alive still in his mind. It was a small solace.

And yet...

They were *free*. Khale was alive, against every odd.

Konrad shifted in his seat, eyes on Weston as he pulled Khale into a hopeful embrace. "Alright," he asked Weston. "Where are we headed?"

From his pocket, Weston withdrew a palm-sized compass, weighted enough that it must have been gold. The face had only the needle, no directions to mark the space around them. Konrad had never set eyes on it before, but Weston held it with great care as the needle settled.

"North, to Paisca," Weston stated, as though he'd known this for some time. He probably had.

To the felucca then and across the sea to Paisca. It was a hospitable land good for farming.

"Three bedrooms?" Khale asked, mind perfectly aligned with Konrad's as it always seemed to be. "And our dog..."

"And our promises," Konrad reminded him.

With a smile, Khale kissed Konrad. It was a kiss of freedom and future. "Fair winds and calm seas," he decided.

Konrad held him, for now and ever. "And a compass to guide the way."

CHARACTERS

Weston Akhan (James Nukoin): A Luck/Earth fae from Wyvern, 17 years old

Konrad Selig: A Gancanagh from the Stilts. His partner is Khale

Casek: Magne's partner
Daxon
Goran: Gunnar's partner
Gunnar: Fire fae, Goran's partner
Khale: Konrad's partner
Marn
Magne: Casek's partner
Oain
Urial
Vas
Weyblor

Ambrose Selig: Konrad's great uncle
Deyton
Florian: 600 years older than Konrad
Negash
Tomlin

ACKNOWLEDGMENTS

EDITOR
JMB EDITING SERVICES

Thank you for your time and feedback.

ALPHA READER

Thank you *A. W. Wang, author of the Ten Sigma Series* for your continued help with the sanding and polishing of our stories.

BETA READER

Thank you *Penny Sue* for your first impressions.

THE ELESARA SERIES

Thank you for supporting our project.

For more, visit our website

www.theelesaraseries.com

HOLLY GRAF

Holly has always loved writing and stories. She surrounds herself in them, in whatever medium possible. She has a passion for fantasy romance and co-authors The Elesara Series. When she isn't writing, she spends her time with her high school sweetheart, two children, and many pets.

HOLLYGRAF.COM

KRISSY MAY

Krissy lives in a chaos factory, which is run by a merciless team of miniature humans and their pets. She enjoys music, foreign languages, noise-cancelling headphones, and the smell of fresh-mowed grass. She has a useless degree in Physics and part of another useless degree in Nursing, neither of which helped in the creation of this book. You can see her co-authored web series War of the Wicca.

KRISSYMAY.COM

Made in the USA
Middletown, DE
08 September 2023

37686734R00118